Praise for

Escape from Aleppo

★ "Filled with kindness and hope, but also with the harsh realities of the horrors of war, this heartbreaking book is a necessary reminder of what many people live through every day."
—*Booklist* (starred review)

". . . [A] valuable introduction to the issues plaguing modern Syria and the costs of war in historically rich locales." —*Kirkus Reviews*

"Senzai crafts a harrowing novel . . . that captures the reality of the conflict while illuminating the culture and history of the country. . . . [T]he novel's taut pacing and memorable heroine result in a gripping and intense story of the traumas inflicted on Syria's citizens." —*Publishers Weekly*

Also by N. H. Senzai

Shooting Kabul

Saving Kabul Corner

Ticket to India

ESCAPE FROM ALEPPO

N. H. Senzai

A Paula Wiseman Book

Simon & Schuster Books for Young Readers

NEW YORK LONDON TORONTO SYDNEY NEW DELHI

SIMON & SCHUSTER BOOKS FOR YOUNG READERS
An imprint of Simon & Schuster Children's Publishing Division
1230 Avenue of the Americas, New York, New York 10020

For information about special discounts for bulk purchases,
please contact Simon & Schuster Special Sales at
1-866-506-1949 or business@simonandschuster.com.
The Simon & Schuster Speakers Bureau can bring authors to your live event. For more information or to book an event, contact the Simon & Schuster Speakers Bureau at 1-866-248-3049 or visit our website at www.simonspeakers.com.
Also available in a Simon & Schuster Books for Young Readers hardcover edition
Cover design by Krista Vossen
Interior design by Hilary Zarycky
The text for this book was set in Stempel Schneider.
Manufactured in the United States of America
0420 OFF
First Simon & Schuster Books for Young Readers paperback edition May 2020
2 4 6 8 10 9 7 5 3 1
The Library of Congress has cataloged the hardcover edition as follows:
Names: Senzai, N. H., author.
Title: Escape from Aleppo / N.H. Senzai.
Description: First Edition. | New York : Simon & Schuster Books for Young Readers, [2018] | "A Paula Wiseman Book." | Summary: After Nadia is separated from her family while fleeing the civil war, she spends the next four days with a mysterious old man who helps her navigate the checkpoints and snipers of the rebel, ISIS, and Syrian armies that are littering Aleppo on her way to meeting her father at the Turkish border.
Identifiers: LCCN 2017015130| ISBN 9781481472173 (hardback)
ISBN 978-1-4814-7218-0 (pbk) | ISBN 9781481472197 (ebook)
Subjects: | CYAC: Refugees—Fiction. | Secrets—Fiction. | Aleppo (Syria)—Fiction. | Syria—History—Civil War, 2011—Fiction. | BISAC: JUVENILE FICTION / Historical / Middle East. | JUVENILE FICTION / People & Places / Middle East. | JUVENILE FICTION / Historical / Military & Wars.
Classification: LCC PZ7.S47953 Es 2018 | DDC [Fic]—dc23 LC record available at https://lccn.loc.gov/2017015130

For the people of Syria: those who stayed,
the countless who fled, and, sadly,
the ones who perished

Chapter One

October 9, 2013   4:37 a.m.

It was neither the explosions, the clatter of running feet, nor the shouting that woke her. Because, as on most nights, Nadia was oblivious to the world, huddled beneath her bed, barricaded under a mound of blankets. Curled up beside her lay Mishmish, his purr in her ear, along with a cold, wet nose. It was her cousin Razan who finally roused her, by dragging her out from under the bed by her stockinged foot.

"Nadia, you oaf, wake up," she hissed, voice tight with fear. In her other hand, she held a sputtering candle. The warm light bobbed in the cold, dark room, illuminating Razan's pale, delicate features, making her appear younger than her twenty-four years.

"What?" mumbled Nadia, gazing bleary-eyed at the window, boarded up with wooden planks. Around the edges she could see nothing but inky darkness. They were supposed to wake as the call for *fajr* prayers rang out in melodious Arabic, before the first light of dawn.

"Get your things, we have to go," ordered Razan, placing the candle on the desk.

"But we don't leave till the morning," grumbled Nadia. Then she heard it. A deep boom in the distance. She froze. That was no familiar call to prayer. "No, no, no! Make it go away," she breathed, eyes squeezed shut.

Fear curled through her belly. Her ears homed in on the echoes, imagining them as waves that rippled from a stone thrown into a pond. With lightning speed, her mind calculated the vibrations back to the point of the bomb's impact, a skill she'd perfected since the war began. She imagined a narrow, thin-lipped face peering at her with a raised eyebrow. *Ms. Darwish.* How her algebra teacher would smirk if she found out that Nadia could now solve complex math problems in her head. Less than two years ago, her teacher had written in her report card that although Nadia was a bright student, she didn't apply herself.

The report card had horrified Nadia's mother, who, it turned out, had been a childhood friend of Ms. Darwish's. They'd attended the same school growing up, but had lost track of one another after graduation. Nadia had flippantly replied that she wasn't interested in algebra nor most of her other subjects—which were boring—except music, drama, and sometimes history: not the tedious dates, of course, but the fascinating, swashbuckling stories of kings and pirates. Her mother had ended up making an appointment with Ms. Darwish to address Nadia's surly attitude and lackluster performance.

Nadia pulled the blanket over her head, wanting to burrow back in time and magically emerge at school, even if it was algebra class. Huddled in the back row with her best friends, they could joke about the rumors of how Ms. Darwish had spurned marriage in order to dedicate her life to teaching her beloved algebra. The passion for her subject, they firmly believed, extended to the man who'd invented it, Muhammad ibn Musa al-Khwarizmi, whose soulful portrait hung in the classroom.

"Don't lie there, you harebrained hamster," Razan yelled, giving her a well-placed kick in the backside.

Nadia grunted, the pain bringing her back to reality. The explosion was from a *barmeela*, a merciless barrel bomb packed with shrapnel, dumped from helicopters onto the rebel-held areas. It was a favorite of the Syrian army. This one had detonated nearly a mile away, Nadia had calculated, likely reducing its target to rubble. Her mouth ran dry as the memory of a similar bomb rose within her, the one that had left the deep scar from her knee to her hip. *I can't go out there,* she thought. She crawled back toward the security under her bed.

"Oh no you don't," growled Razan, grabbing her leg. "This is not the time for you to play ostrich."

"But . . . ," cried Nadia, heart-racing panic building in her chest.

Razan grabbed her face and held it close to hers. "I know you're scared, but you have to focus," she said fiercely. "We've practiced this and all you need to do is exit the front door. I'll drag you the rest of the way!"

Reluctantly, Nadia nodded, teeth clenched. Razan hurried toward the heavy wooden armoire. "Get your things—we don't have time to waste."

Nadia crawled toward the corner of her room where she'd put her backpack, filled days before, and double-checked to make sure her little pink case was inside. She pulled on her threadbare winter coat, running her finger across the silver pin, shaped like a fallen-over 8, fixed near the collar, then slipped on thick woolen mittens. She grabbed the special burlap case she'd spent weeks sewing, with the help of Nana, who was always there to find a solution to her problems.

"Amani!" *Khala* Fatima bellowed out Nadia's mother's name. "Get the kids—we have to go!"

Nadia could imagine Khala Fatima standing at the front door of her apartment, down the hall from theirs, her face red with exertion, her stocky figure enveloped in a flowing gray dress. She'd given up her favorite oranges, pinks, and yellows when snipers had taken roost atop deserted buildings, looking for targets, which more often than not ended up being defenseless women and children. Now it was best to blend in with the drab concrete wasteland that the city had become. But what her aunt said next made her blood run cold.

"Malik thinks the helicopters are coming this way."

Malik was her cousin and Khala Fatima's eldest, and he and Nadia frequently butted heads, especially when he was being a bossy know-it-all. But if he'd actually seen helicopters . . . She flew into action, despite the fear dragging down her limbs. She reached beneath the bed, pulled out Mishmish, and held the comforting mass of white-and-orange fur for a moment. Found as a newborn, the kitten had been kept alive by Razan, who'd applied her veterinary skills. In a way, Mishmish had given life back to Razan, who'd been lost in a well of grief after her husband was killed in a bombing at the university where they'd both been studying. The kitten had grown fat and sleek, and to Nadia's consternation, because she didn't like animals, little kids, dirt, or disruptions, the cat decided Nadia was his. He followed her around, slept on her bed, ate off her plate when she wasn't looking, and brought her special treats of dead mice.

The cat allowed himself to be secreted away inside a burlap bag and lay curled along Nadia's side when she slung the bag over her shoulder. She grabbed her pack and followed Razan, candle in hand, from the room. "Let's go," said her cousin.

You can do this . . . you can do this . . . , repeated the voice inside Nadia's head. According to the emergency plan, her grandmother, mother, and three aunts and their children were to assemble downstairs within two minutes of an alert.

They hurried down the dark hall of the spacious apartment that had been Nadia's home her entire life.

It was identical to the other three apartments in the building, built by her grandparents thirty-five years ago. Each son had been given the key to his own flat, while they occupied the top floor. Mostly, they'd all lived happily together in the rambling space as part of a large extended family. Overwhelmed by the thought that she was leaving the only home she'd known, she tripped on her shoelaces. Instantly a sharp pain shot up her leg and she gritted her teeth. She paused to rub her leg where the pain had flared, near her knee, a few inches from where a sliver of shrapnel still lay buried.

"Tie your shoelaces," grumbled Razan, adjusting her bag.

"Are you girls ready?" came a breathless voice from the master bedroom. It was Nadia's mother.

"Yes," said Razan.

"Go on downstairs," urged Nadia's mother, now in the hall. "Razan, help Nadia," she added. "And, Nadia, stay with Razan and listen to what she says—no arguments!"

Nadia grimaced. Razan's job was to make sure she didn't get *stuck*.

"Don't worry," said Razan, latching onto Nadia's arm. "Aren't you coming?"

"Just another minute," responded Nadia's mother. "Yusuf can't find his shoes."

Nadia frowned. Her younger brother was always a pain. "We'll wait for you," she grumbled, lips twisting downward.

"No," said her mother, eyes stern. "You go, I'm right behind you."

Reluctantly, Nadia let her cousin propel her toward the front door.

Her brother's wail echoed behind them. "I don't want the red ones," he fussed. "They're too tight. Where are the blue ones?"

"We can't find them now," came her mother's patient voice as they exited the apartment and stepped out onto the third-floor landing.

"The helicopters are circling back!" came Malik's bellow from above.

Nadia imagined him somewhere on the balcony, looking out over the night sky with his binoculars. Her throat tightened at the thought of leaving. She had barely stepped outside their building in over a year . . . not since the day she'd been hit by a *barmeela*. *I can't do this,* she thought. *I can't go back out there. . . .*

Chapter Two

October 9, 2013   5:03 a.m.

"Come on, everyone!" shouted Khala Fatima, exiting her apartment, dressed head to toe in a dreary gray as Nadia had predicted. "You girls okay?" she asked.

As Razan nodded, Nana floated out next, a sprightly figure in black. Tucked beneath a forest-green scarf, her grandmother's once rich brown hair had gone white practically overnight when Nadia's grandfather, *Jiddo*, had died of a stroke and her sons had left for war. With a calm smile on her elegant features, she gave Nadia an encouraging smile and led the little kids, who marched in practiced, military precision, toward the stairs. One of them started sobbing.

"Now, now, my heart, don't cry." Nana's soothing voice drifted up from the stairwell. "We're going on an adventure, you'll see. Soon we'll be somewhere safe.

And maybe we'll find some chocolate—what do you think about that?"

Safe. What does that feel like? Nadia thought, her heart racing as she stood on the landing, clutching the banister till her knuckles shone white. *Chocolate.* She remembered her birthday cake, her taste buds recalling the creamy, sweet goodness.

Razan turned to Nadia. "Come on," she said encouragingly. "You can do this. We've practiced it over a hundred times."

With a gulp, she followed her cousin down the marble steps and caught the comforting whiff of her grandmother's soap: a calming, earthy fragrance of laurel oil. Khala Lina came into view, standing in front of her apartment with her twin boys, dressed in threadbare woolen pants, button-down shirts, and too-small cardigans their father had purchased on a trip to London long ago. Khala Lina always insisted that they look their best, even in the midst of a war. Silk scarf tied in place over her hair, lips marked with a touch of pink lipstick, she looked as if she were on her way to work at the hospital to deliver a set of triplets. But regardless of how much she irritated Nadia, especially after she'd blamed Nadia for her own injury—*like I wanted to get hit by a bomb*—it was Khala Lina who'd saved her leg by removing most of the shrapnel, except for that one piece, and given her painkillers to control the pain. "Has everyone come down?" Nadia asked Khala Lina.

"Khala Amani is behind us," replied Razan as they continued down.

Nana kept an eye on the kids in the lobby while Razan's mother, Khala Shakira, stood apart, staring out the front door into the darkness. Even with all the chaos surrounding them, her soft golden eyes seemed vacant. They'd been that way since the day Razan's father had disappeared, taken away by the *mukhabarat*, the government's secret police. Just thinking of the shadowy figures in their black leather jackets sent a shiver of fear through Nadia. Every day, her aunt had sat at the window, expecting him to come home.

"Mama, stop," cried Razan, running toward her mother, who'd pulled open the front door, as if to walk out.

Nadia stood separate from the kids, hidden within the shadows of the staircase, and eavesdropped on her other aunts.

"What do we do?" whispered Khala Fatima to Khala Lina, checking the blank screen of her mobile phone with a frown. "We can't get ahold of the men. The phones still aren't working. Neither is the Internet, so I can't send an e-mail either." She shoved it back into her purse, her face now as gray as her dress.

"We stick to the original plan," said Khala Lina with authority. "We were going to meet them at the dental clinic at noon. Now we'll just get there a few hours early."

Nadia remembered the night her father and uncles had made a rare appearance at home, a few weeks back. Huddled over a meager meal, they'd shared the news that the war was not going well. The Syrian army had recaptured Khanasir, the city on the main road into Aleppo, or Haleb as it was known to locals. The rumor on the streets was that a major siege was coming. Though it broke their hearts, they'd decided that the family had to leave, before the next wave of death and destruction battered the city.

Where are the men? thought Nadia, hand trembling as she unconsciously patted the cat. *I hope they're all right.* Her mind raced, praying her father, older brothers, and uncles were on their way to the dental clinic.

A circle of bright light shone from atop the staircase, distracting her. It was followed by Malik's feet. He careened down the steps and stood panting at the bottom. "It's coming this way . . . we have to go now!"

Nadia's aunts stood frozen, staring at each other, until Khala Lina flew into action. She ran up the stairs, shouting, "Amani, where are you? We have to go!"

What's taking Mama so long? Nadia fumed. *Yusuf and his stupid shoes.* The kids screamed as an explosion reverberated from up the street; then they started bawling in earnest. Nadia did the mental math. The helicopters were in the street parallel to theirs, a quarter of a mile away.

Malik wiped a sheen of sweat from his forehead as silence descended over the lobby. Khala Fatima had just opened her mouth when they heard her mother call out, "We're coming." Footsteps rang out against the stairs as her mother descended, shouldering a bulky bag and carrying Yusuf, wearing his too-tight red shoes. Obviously, they hadn't found the other pair.

Anxiety bubbled through Nadia, coupled with anger, an emotion that seemed to accompany her everywhere these days, especially when things didn't go her way. And in the last few years, it seemed that everything that could go wrong had. Even though she tried to push the awful feelings away, she couldn't help but hate everything: her stupid little brother, the fact that they had little to eat, the loss of her previous life, the stupid war . . . everything.

"We should avoid the front door and use the back," said Malik, leading the way.

But we're supposed to use the front door, thought Nadia, legs tense. *That's the plan. That's what we practiced.* Her anxiety worsening, she trailed behind the others as they hurried through the hall that ended at the back door.

Having passed through the doorway, the group descended a series of steps. Nadia watched everyone run across the carport, past the dusty old Jeep, parked parallel to the steps. The men had taken the truck, and Jiddo's gleaming sedan had been stolen long ago. Without repairs or gasoline, the Jeep and two other cars sat useless. Even if they had been operational, it was too dangerous to maneuver through the city, avoiding helicopters, militias, and checkpoints.

Outside. I have to get outside, thought Nadia, finally registering that she was alone. *Where's Razan?* Panic blossomed in her chest as she glimpsed her cousin with her mother. Nadia inched toward the back door, legs trembling. Chill autumn air caressed her hot cheeks as her fingers reached to grip the doorframe. She pulled herself through the opening and paused to catch her breath. *Nearly there.* Malik's flashlight bobbed in the distance, illuminating a path through the cars. Nadia's aunts herded the little ones between them, urging them to be silent as they gathered at the back gate.

Razan stumbled to a stop, then looked around. "Wait!" she cried out. "Where is Nadia?" An arc of light bounced back toward the apartment building, careening from the rusty old Jeep to Nadia, who raised her hand to shield her eyes. The whir of the helicopter's blades sounded in the distance, signaling its approach.

"Why is she just standing there?" came Khala Lina's irritated voice. "Does she want to kill herself? Kill us all?"

"Nadia, you need to hurry!" pleaded her mother.

"Sweetheart, don't be afraid," added Nana. "Come down, I know you can do it."

ıl get her," said Razan, about to run back.

Malik grabbed her arm. "No, let me," he said.

Not that fool Malik, thought Nadia, embarrassed. With a grunt, she heaved herself forward just as the wind above them shifted. The helicopter, she realized in horror, was looming just beyond their apartment building. Nadia stalled, a memory flashing back, of another helicopter . . . another bomb.

"Please, go," cried Malik, waving at the rest of the family, huddled at the back gate. "I'll get Nadia and meet you on the corner, near Shawarma King restaurant."

But the women stood at the back gate, indecision flooding their faces. Nadia stared as Malik raced toward her, but before he was halfway to the Jeep, a shuddering thud hit their building. A deafening roar reverberated through the air as the right corner of their roof shattered and came tumbling down. The force of the explosion sent Nadia tumbling down the steps. Her forehead slammed against the Jeep's bumper and she lay there, ears ringing, blinded by the cloud of dust.

"Nadia!" cried Malik as a plume of gray powder filled the air.

"Where is she?" shouted her mother. "I don't see her!"

"Malik!" she heard Razan scream. "Find her!"

"Nadia, where are you?" cried Malik, his voice muffled as the left wall of the apartment complex crumbled in an avalanche of dust and debris.

"Ya Allah!" cried Nana, her voice echoing.

"She's not here!" shouted Malik, coughing. "All I see is rubble."

"Was she hit?" shouted one of her aunts.

"She . . . she's under the rubble!" shouted Malik.

"Is she alive?" someone shouted.

"I don't know," cried Malik.

"The helicopter, it's still circling back!" screamed Khala Fatima.

I'm here, thought Nadia, lying at the bottom of the last step, stuck between the curb and the side of the Jeep. But as she tried to rise, she saw a metal canister fall from the sky and hit their neighbor's apartment complex as if in slow motion. She watched it explode, engulfing the top floor in flames. Fiery debris rained out into their carport, accompanied by horrified screams. A hot scrap of metal landed on Nadia's arm, forcing her from her stupor. *Move!* screamed a voice in her head. Smoke and ash surrounded her. Instinctively, she crawled under the Jeep, escaping the growing heat from the flames.

"They're pushing out another bomb," cried Khala Lina. "We have to go."

"She can't be dead!" came her mother's anguished wail.

"We can't leave her," sobbed Razan.

"If we stay, we're all going to die!" shouted Khala Lina.

Nana's strong voice rose above the rest. "I don't believe it—she is alive. . . . Find her!"

No, don't leave me! thought Nadia, her head throbbing as she drifted in and out of consciousness, staring at the flickering flames. . . .

Chapter Three

December 17, 2010

Light blazed from a dozen white candles atop a towering chocolate cake. Adorned with pink sugar roses, the cake was from Nadia's favorite bakery, Palmyra Boulangerie. Her mother set it on the dining table, and Nadia imagined layers of vanilla cake, and raspberry jam beneath the swirls of chocolate buttercream. Even though she was stuffed from the feast that Nana and her mother had prepared, including her favorite, *kabob karaz*, grilled lamb meatballs prepared with cherries and pine nuts, she'd saved room for a slice, maybe even two.

This is definitely one of the best days of my life, she thought happily. Her family and friends from school, along with her parents' friends and neighbors, gathered in her grandparents' elegant dining room. Nadia stood at the center of attention, fiddling with the sash of the satin aquamarine dress. The moment she'd seen it at the store, she'd pleaded with her father to buy it for her; and he had, claiming that the color of the dress matched her eyes so perfectly, it was meant for her. She had painted her nails a similar shade of blue as well. Knife in hand, she moved closer to the table, basking in the compliment her best friend, Rima, had given her when she'd arrived.

Wow, you look just like Carmen!

Later, when Nadia had caught a glimpse of herself in the hall mirror, she'd agreed; her upswept dark hair was in a style identical to the one worn by the gorgeous semifinalist from *Arab Idol,* Carmen Suleiman. And now that her mother had finally relented, she'd gotten the birthday present she had been dying for, singing lessons from Ms. Hussain, who lived down the street.

She spotted Ms. Darwish hovering in the corner like a crow, a guest of her mother's, laughing with her aunt. Nadia had overheard that her mother and Nana were going to introduce her teacher to an eligible bachelor they'd invited as well, but he hadn't shown up yet. They were ready to sing "Happy Birthday," when *Ammo* Zayn, Razan's father, called from the living room. "*Baba*, brothers, you need to see this."

Nadia frowned, wondering what in the world was so important that it had to interrupt this critical part of her special day. The candles sputtered, threatening to ruin the cake with melted wax. With a huff, she allowed her friends to sing so she could blow them out. While her mother cut slices and her friends admired her stack of presents, she slipped into the living room. She found the men and Khala Lina riveted to the television.

Nadia's irritated gaze settled on the well-known anchorwoman from Syria One News, Sara Aloush, with her bright red lipstick and sharp bob. The shot cut to a young reporter in an ill-fitting suit standing near an overturned vegetable cart on a dusty street. A crowd milled in front of a white building, windows framed by turquoise shutters.

"I'm standing in front of the provincial headquarters of a small town called Sidi Bouzid, in Tunisia, in North Africa," said the reporter. "At this site, a young man, Mohamed Bouazizi, poured gasoline over his body and set himself on fire."

Nadia frowned. *Why would he do that?* she thought, intrigued by the gruesome story, momentarily forgetting her irritation.

"It's being reported that he did this to protest years of harassment and humiliation at the hands of corrupt government officials, who recently confiscated his vegetable cart."

The reporter stopped a portly mustached man and asked, "Did you know Bouazizi?"

Eyes earnest, the man looked into the camera. "No, not personally, but he was like thousands of other young men across Tunisia, struggling with limited job prospects."

"Back to you, Sara," said the reporter. The camera cut back to the news desk.

"We have been able to locate the Bouazizi family," said Sara, leaning forward at her desk so that her bobbed hair fell across her cheeks.

The screen shifted to a tiny woman, her round face framed by a pink scarf, tears running down her cheeks. She stood in a cramped one-room apartment, surrounded by half a dozen people. "My nephew's dream was to save enough money to buy a truck to help with his work," she said. "He was so tired when he came home after pushing his vegetable cart all day. That cart was his livelihood. He was the breadwinner for our family. Now he's dead at only twenty-six."

Ammo Zayn shared a worried look with Nadia's father. "This will have consequences," he murmured.

Khala Lina leapt from the sofa and shuttered the windows, her lips pressed together. Words had a way of drifting into the wrong ears, Nadia knew. From the corner of her eye, she saw Ms. Darwish standing at the door, a worried look on her face.

"No, no," said Jiddo, her grandfather, shaking his grizzled white head. "It's just a local issue of unemployment."

She glanced at Jiddo's stern expression. He firmly believed that if you stayed out of trouble and worked hard, as he had done, you would lead a successful, peaceful life. At least once a month, he lectured her and her cousins on how his family had lived in a two-room flat in the Old City and didn't have enough money for him to finish high school. And how, at fourteen, he'd gone to work at one of the phosphate mines that dotted the northeastern part of Syria. With hard work and the grace of *Allah*, he'd built a successful chemical fertilizer business. He'd puff out his chest and tell them that his sons had all gone on to college, including Nadia's father, a chemical engineer, who now helped run the business.

"Zayn may be right, Baba," said Nadia's father, a frown creasing his forehead. "Yes, it's about unemployment, but this young man's death may have opened an old wound that has been festering for a long time."

"But he shouldn't have killed himself, it solves nothing," said Jiddo, eyes troubled. "To take one's life is a great sin."

"Yes," agreed Ammo Zayn, "but it looks like he snapped from the frustration and humiliation . . . and people are taking notice."

Nadia slunk back to her party and stood by the window, the story of the young man still on her mind.

Ms. Darwish found her and slipped a small box into her hand. "Open it," she said. Inside lay a heavy silver pin, shaped liked a sideways 8.

"It's beautiful," said Nadia, surprised by the gift and the warmth in her teacher's usually stern face.

"In algebra it's called the lemniscate, the symbol for infinity. It's a never-ending loop that conveys unlimited possibilities. I have high expectations for you, Nadia, my dear, that you can accomplish great things if you put your mind to it."

"Thank you," murmured Nadia, suddenly weighed down by Ms. Darwish's words. As her teacher disappeared into the living room, Nadia took the large slice of cake she'd been looking forward to and stood with her friends, who were having an animated discussion about their plans for the approaching holidays. But as she sucked on a pink sugar rose, she thought of the young man who'd killed himself, and the sweetness turned bitter.

As her father had predicted, others did take notice of Bouazizi's fiery end. His death brought to boil the long-simmering anger burning within Tunisians. They took to the streets in what became known as the Jasmine Revolution. Furious about the level of corruption within the government, they demanded jobs, food, and better living conditions, while pushing for freedom and political reforms. Dozens died in clashes with government forces. But for Nadia, thoughts of the vegetable vendor and a small town in Tunisia soon evaporated. She had too many important things going on in her life: *Arab Idol* finals were coming up and her friends were betting on whether their favorite singers would win. Plus, her cousin Razan needed help planning her wedding, which was scheduled for April, at one of the swankiest hotels in town. Exams were also on the horizon and her mother was hounding her to study, which was a total pain. She'd do fine in literature, history, and drama, but in her gut, she knew she was going to do terribly in algebra, no matter what Ms. Darwish said.

Chapter Four

October 9, 2013   4:08 p.m.

Pain. Deep throbbing pain rippled from Nadia's toes to her head, where a pounding headache raged, radiating from a lump on her forehead. Her eyelids, caked with dust, ached as they flickered open. For a moment, she thought she was back in her room, cocooned beneath her bed. Then the memories flooded back: *exiting the apartment . . . the helicopter . . .* bar-meela *falling from the sky . . . the explosions and fire . . .* Her vision sharpened and she took in the metal guts of her uncle's old Jeep. It had saved her life. Panic blossomed in her heart and she froze, her ears probing for sounds. But there was no whir of helicopter blades, no thud of bombs. No voices. Only silence.

Cautiously, she rolled out from beneath the car, squinting against the light. The sun hung low in the sky, partially obscured by a cover of dark clouds.

With shaky legs, she leaned against the Jeep, amazed that she'd survived another bomb attack. But all relief evaporated as she stared at what remained of her home. By some miracle, the left side of the building still stood, but the right, along with their neighbor's apartment building, had been reduced to rubble, then charred by fire. She peered inside Khala Lina's apartment, cut in half, her embroidered silk curtains still hanging from the window, fluttering like a maroon flag. A leather sofa hung from the ledge, its matching love seat lying on what remained of Khala Fatima's kitchen below, her stove flat as an *atayaf*, a sweet cheese-stuffed pancake. Nana's beautiful cream-and-gold china lay scattered across the ground like snowflakes, broken in a million pieces. Tears slipped down Nadia's cheeks. *It's all gone.* Anguish morphed into rage. *And my family is gone. How could they?* An unforgiving hardness settled like a jagged stone near her heart.

Get ahold of yourself, said a voice inside her head. *This is no time to fall apart. You must find the others.*

She thought back to the moment the bomb struck, sending her tumbling down the steps. Malik had been looking for her, but she'd crawled under the car. *They thought I was hit . . . that I was dead.* Her fury deflated like a punctured balloon. She took a ragged breath, trying to sort her jumbled thoughts. *Think. What do I do?* She didn't have a phone. Even if she did, it would be useless since the government had disrupted telecommunications networks and access to the Internet.

Anxiety pooled in her chest, but she shoved it away, trying to remember the route to Dr. Asbahi's dental clinic. She'd visited last year, to get a cavity filled. Her mother had driven north, past the soccer stadium, then she'd cut east, past Bilal Mosque. The clinic was a few blocks from there, but that part was a bit fuzzy. *I'll find it. Then I'm going to give Malik a piece of my mind for making everyone think I was dead under the rubble.*

She glanced down at her watch as a siren wailed in the distance. *Four o'clock. They were supposed to meet the men at noon!* She buttoned her coat and turned toward the back gate. Old fears came rushing back. *No . . . no . . . I can't go out there.*

You can and you will, came a voice from deep inside, now sounding remarkably like Ms. Darwish.

Okay, I can do this, she repeated over and over again

in her head, running her fingers along the silver pin. Then something else sparked her memory. *Missing . . . something's missing.* She bent down and peered under the car. It wasn't her backpack she was interested in, but the burlap sack. It lay on the cracked steps, suspiciously flat. *Empty.*

"Mishmish!" croaked Nadia, searching for a flash of orange and white. "Where are you, you dumb cat?" Desperately, she scrambled through the wreckage, but there was no flash of marmalade fur. The cat that never used to leave her side, and could always sniff her out, had disappeared. He'd probably been scared out of his wits and run away, she realized, shoulders sinking. "He's just a stupid cat. Who needs him anyway?" she growled, eyes hot with unshed tears. She reluctantly turned to the back gate. Cold wind swirled past, leaving her exposed beneath the slate gray sky. She realized that if she kept her eyes down and didn't look around too much, she could keep the fear at bay. *Don't think. Just move.* She secured her bags over her shoulder and staggered toward the back gate.

Nadia's neighborhood, Salaheddine, sat in southwestern Aleppo on the front lines of the battle. It was caught in a tug-of-war between the government and rebel forces. And despite the fact that months of conflict had reduced much of the district to rubble, to Nadia it was still as familiar as the back of her hand. Her brothers, her cousins, and neighborhood kids had spent countless hours prowling the back streets, playing and causing mischief. Shoving aside memories of happier times, she focused on the clinic, which had been a ten-minute drive away. *Well, it used to be.* She recalled from her aunt's whispers over the past week. *We need to go slow, be careful and stay out of sight from both rebels and government forces. It might take two hours to reach the clinic.* Khala Lina's words rang in her ears.

Nadia was struck by the eerie silence as she made her way through the streets, which were beginning to fill with people rushing to finish errands before taking cover. Aleppo had been a big, bustling city, but ever since the conflict began, those who could afford to had left. And in the last few weeks, news had come of President Bashar al-Assad's desire to crush the strengthening opposition in the city. The number of *barmeela* had doubled, even tripled, as the Syrian army reinforced its position. As a result, the city was split, with the government in control of the northwest while rebels maintained positions in the southeast.

Rebels, snorted Nadia. An image of her father, brothers, uncles, and cousins flashed in her mind. Peaceful, hardworking men. *Not so-called rebels . . . enemies of the state.* The ever-simmering pool of anger bubbled up again, spurring her past houses where shells had punched great holes and others that had collapsed completely, blocking the surrounding alleys with rubble. On the corner, her music teacher's house looked fine except for a hole in the roof, which had spurred her and her family to flee months before. A face peered down at her from the top floor. Squatters, families looking for a safe place to hide out. Behind her, a wailing ambulance approached, emblazoned with a red crescent, and seconds later came a dusty truck, filled with men and women in white helmets. Nadia had heard about these volunteers who rushed to bomb sites to help victims. Both vehicles pulled up beside a smoldering structure a few blocks ahead. Nadia faltered as she heard cries of anguish. She approached the ruins of what had been a large apartment complex, now a stack of concrete pancakes with jagged metal rods protruding from all angles.

Survivors huddled near the road, coated in dust, consoling the injured while paramedics bandaged a boy's leg. An old man knelt beside the rubble, weeping, his bent figure shielding something. Nadia got a glimpse of golden bangles and a frail arm. With a gulp, she jerked her gaze away, spotting a group of women clawing through the wreckage, shoving aside broken furniture.

"Sisters, gently," cried a woman in a white helmet as she and the others in the truck assembled their equipment. "You don't want to bring more of the building down."

"My baby is in there!" cried a young woman, her eyes wild.

Stretcher held high, the volunteers ran to an overhanging stretch of concrete and motioned everyone to be quiet. And as an eerie silence fell over the area, Nadia heard it, a plaintive wail to the left of where the woman stood. With quick movements, one of the men dug into the rubble, just above the source of the crying. He handed back a broken television and lay down so he could reach into the narrow hole. Nadia held her breath as he stretched into the crevice while another volunteer held on to his legs.

"*Alhamdulillah*, praise be to God!" he cried, rearing up, a bundle in his hands. The baby's magnificent wail filled the silence as he handed the child to her mother.

Nadia exhaled in a rush, relieved at the happy ending. She glanced back toward home, hoping to see a familiar feline form. Disappointed, she kept her eyes on the ground and hurried on, stepping over a pair of shattered eyeglasses.

Once past Al-Hamadaniah Stadium, home to Al-Hurriya, her brother's favorite soccer team, Nadia paused behind a broken-down truck to catch her breath and orient herself. Again she looked behind her, hoping to see a cat running up the street, tail held high. *Nothing.* She veered across a wide street, making herself as small as possible, limping past huddled groups of people. She didn't make eye contact with anyone, and no one paid much attention to a lone girl flitting past them like a shadow.

Through a network of quieter alleys, reeking with uncollected trash, she continued north, halting at an intersection leading to a small square. A torn banner hung from a lamppost. GOD, SYRIA, AND BASHAR ALONE! it read. Another one lay near her feet, proclaiming, WITH OUR BLOOD AND OUR SOULS WE SHALL SACRIFICE OURSELVES FOR YOU, O BASHAR!

She inched back and caught sight of a group of men in military fatigues, lounging behind a row of barrels blocking the road. Metal glinted from holsters hanging from their shoulders. *Rifles.* Nadia gulped, remembering her father talking about the hundreds of checkpoints that had sprung up around the city, each manned by a different group, either affiliated with the Syrian army or one of the hundreds of rebel groups. One thing they all had in common was that they held you up, checked for identification cards, and interrogated you. If they didn't like your answers, you could be beaten . . . or worse. Fear crept along the edges of her mind, weighing down her limbs. She eyed an empty juice stall, broken blenders littering the counter. *I could just rest there for a bit. . . .*

No you don't, reprimanded a voice inside her head. *Keep moving.*

Teeth gritted, she scurried back along the alley and merged onto a side street. Shadowy faces stared down at her from apartment buildings that lined both sides of the street, remarkably untouched by the bullets and bomb blasts. As she neared the end of the street, she heard a plaintive meow and stopped, filled with hope. But it was a blue-eyed Siamese yowling from atop a fence.

Disappointed, she rounded the corner, then froze. In front of her was a familiar shopwindow. Through dirty, cracked glass she saw a room painted powder pink. Memories flooded back: *her first haircut while sitting primly on a purple leather chair; manicures with her cousins and aunts; Razan's image reflected in the glittering mirror, a white veil over a fancy hairdo for her wedding.* But now, Caramel Salon stood abandoned, its stylish owner, Christine, long gone, along with the bottles of coconut-scented shampoo, henna conditioners, hair sprays, pomades, and latest colors of nail polish—Vermillion, Amethyst, and Mink Pink.

A distinct image flared in her mind, of being eight, sitting in a corner as her mother got her hair cut. She'd wandered over to the manicure station to admire the collection of nail polish, each a brilliant shade of fabulous. When she thought no one was looking, she'd slipped a bottle into her pocket. As they'd prepared to leave,

Christine had given her a wink and whispered in her ear, "I hope your nails look pretty—Tangerine Dreams is one of my favorites." Embarrassed, and terrified her mother would find out, she'd tried to give it back, but Christine had told her to keep it. Nadia pulled off one of her mittens and glanced down at her cold hand, soft from Pond's cream, nails painted Dusty Rose.

Her eyes shifted, catching her reflection in the mirror. A stranger stared back at her: face covered in dust, hollowed cheeks marked with pale white scars. A cut, caked with dry blood, from where her head had hit the Jeep. Her hair, once thick and wavy, had been hacked off because of lice. Spiky and short, it now lay stuffed under an ugly olive-green woolen cap that had belonged to her father. It matched the bulky green coat he'd always worn but had forgotten the last time he was home.

Her friend Rima's voice came tauntingly back—*You look just like Carmen!* The singer with the strikingly beautiful features, who'd won *Arab Idol. "Beautiful" is not an adjective anyone would use for me now,* she thought bitterly. Only the eyes were the same, a deep, velvety aquamarine.

Chapter Five

October 9, 2013 5:19 p.m.

Nadia fled. The blocks passed in a blur until her lungs felt like they'd burst. Wheezing, she stopped along the road, doubling over to catch her breath.

"Are you okay, child?" asked an old woman, her lined face burdened by a sadness that so many in the city wore. Nadia nodded, watching the woman and her grandchildren scavenge through the remains of what had been a grocery store. A tiny girl in a ragged dress squealed, holding up a can of *ful*, stewed beans.

Nadia's stomach growled. She couldn't remember when she'd last eaten. She was about to thank the woman for her concern but saw that she was already retreating into the shadows. Nadia looked over her shoulder and spotted a black Mercedes. Inside, men in black leather jackets and sunglasses blew smoke out the rolled-down windows. *Mukhabarat.* Nadia's instinct was to hide, but there was nowhere to go. Bent low, she darted up the street, past rubbish heaps, trying to be as inconspicuous as a mouse.

Her footsteps slowed as she ended up in a cul-de-sac, surrounded by sagging apartments, faint echoes of laughter ricocheting against the walls. *Strange,* she thought. She moved toward a gate between two buildings. The warm glow of bright yellow monkey bars came into view, along with a swing set rigged together with rope, a teeter-totter rusty with age, and a towering pile of sand. It was a sprawling park where a dozen rowdy kids roamed with joyful abandon. Nadia stood perplexed, wondering how they could be out playing in the middle of a war zone. A boy about Yusuf's age, in dirty jeans and a sweater too large for his scrawny frame, walked by, lugging a sloshing plastic bucket.

Water, thought Nadia, licking her parched lips. "Hey," she croaked, hoping to get a cool mouthful. The boy, not hearing her, dragged the bucket over to a series of mounds that bordered the playground. Nadia followed. "Can I get a drink?" she blurted.

The boy paused. "Make it quick, and not too much." He handed her a plastic cup.

Quickly she slurped a full cup of the cool water, and took another to rinse her hands and face before he could complain. As soon as she'd finished, he lugged the bucket over to a mound covered with shards of white stone, and carefully poured water over it. "What are you doing?" she asked.

"I'm watering Mommy," he replied.

Nadia frowned. "Watering your mother?"

He looked at her like that was the kind of idiotic question only outsiders asked. "If I water her, then something will grow for sure, to give her shade."

His mother's grave. "I—I'm sorry," she stammered, eyeing the rows of mounds hugging the playground on all sides.

The boy shrugged. "It was her heart. We wanted to take her to the hospital but it was gone. Destroyed by bombs. We couldn't find anyone to help her in time."

"Hey," cried out a girl in long pigtails, pointing to a fresh mound. "Splash some on the martyrs too."

The boy nodded and poured water on the other graves.

"Martyrs?" Nadia asked.

"They are the men of our neighborhood," he said. "Fighting that dirty *kalb*, Assad."

Nadia couldn't help but look over her shoulder when the boy called President Assad a dog. It was against the law to criticize the government.

"All these people are martyrs?" Nadia asked.

For the second time, the boy looked at her like she was an idiot. "No. They are fathers, cousins, aunts, and sisters."

"Hey, don't water those!" shouted the pigtailed girl, her dirty face red. The boy had neared a section cordoned off with blue rope.

"Who are they?" asked Nadia.

"Shabiha," said the boy.

Nadia's skin crawled. *Shabiha* . . . ghosts. Known for their brutal, unmerciful efficiency, they were armed thugs, loyal only to Assad, carrying out his dirty work. Dressed in black, wearing white trainers, they came in like apparitions and left death in their wake. "Why are they here?" she whispered, not wanting to be near them even if they were dead.

"They got blown up over there," he said, pointing

to the opposite side of the blue rope, a wide section that stretched the length of the playground. "There were three, or maybe four. We couldn't tell since there were so many body parts. But they had to be buried, so the grown-ups dumped sand on them."

"Don't cross that line," said the girl, waving her spatula with authority as she played with dented pots and pans in the sand pit. "That's where they're fighting."

It dawned on Nadia how these kids could play here so openly: The playground lay in a no-man's land. Two blocks beyond the blue line lay government soldiers and snipers. Assad's tanks and helicopters would not bomb here, or they would risk hitting their own men. Rebel forces lay in the other direction. Nadia stared at the graves, feeling sick. Enemies fighting in life were now lying together in death. And interspersed between them were the civilians whose lives they'd turned into ash.

"Jamal!" cried a boy with missing front teeth who was hanging from the monkey bars. He waved at the boy with the bucket. "Let's play Assad's army and rebels."

"I'm a rebel this time!" shouted Jamal, dropping his bucket. He pulled a gun from his pocket, assembled from sticks, twine, and bits of plastic, and struck a pose that again reminded her of her brother, Yusuf.

Her brother . . . "I have to go," she blurted out.

Jamal was about to say something, when a muffled boom rang out in the distance, past the row of apartment buildings. The children froze.

"Mortar," called the girl with the pigtails, and the others nodded.

"Yeah," said the boy with missing teeth. "Definitely not tank rounds."

"Higher pitch," added Jamal.

Like Nadia, these kids recognized the sounds that accompanied death. *Keep moving. It's going to be dark soon.* She stepped out onto the scraggly grass. "Bye," she called out.

A chorus of good-byes sang out behind her as Nadia sprinted in the opposite direction from the blue line, going north. At the edge of the battleground, she clung to a line of sheets that had been hung as a protection against snipers. Before the war, these same sheets had served a very different purpose, providing privacy and protection against the sun. She turned and waved to the kids and slipped into a side street as another mortar rumbled behind her, followed by the warning call from a woman on a balcony, yelling at the kids to come inside.

Chapter Six

October 9, 2013   6:26 p.m.

Dusk licked the edges of the leaden sky, unfurling tendrils of pink and orange along the horizon, sending a shiver of worry through Nadia. Night was quickly approaching, and although the cover of darkness would aid in shrouding her from prying eyes, it would also make it harder for her to see where she was going. She'd left the playground over half an hour ago, all the while searching for familiar landmarks that would help direct her to the mosque. But entire city blocks had been reduced to rubble, and buildings she remembered were scarred and unrecognizable.

Nadia paused to catch her breath at the next intersection, where a makeshift market stood, filled with people selling personal belongings or items they'd somehow procured from outside the city. A woman displayed used clothing and beside her a man hawked a television, stereo, and refrigerator. But in a city without electricity, they were useless. Ignoring the boy trying desperately to sell his bicycle, most congregated around a man presiding over plump vegetables, all at exorbitant sums that few could afford. Nadia stared longingly at a bright red tomato and hurried on.

Finally, she spotted something she knew: the sign for Palmyra Boulangerie. It hung over a desolate shop, its exquisite desserts long gone. Windows shattered, door broken in, its shelves were bare. Once they'd carried the cookies she adored—*armouch*, crunchy cinnamon meringue studded with walnuts. Next door lay the remains of the little stationery shop Razan had loved. Saddened but relieved that she had an idea where she was, Nadia pushed on. Hopefully, she'd soon spot another site that would help guide her.

But twenty minutes later, having passed the car dealership where her uncle had purchased the Jeep that had saved her life, panic bloomed in her heart. *Bilal Mosque shouldn't be this far,* she thought as a terrible certainty set in. *Lost. I'm lost.* She stumbled to a stop in front of an appliance store, its roof caved in, the innards of refrigerators and stoves oozing from all sides. Somewhere, she'd taken a wrong turn. *But where? Maybe I should have taken a right, not a left, after the car dealership,* she thought, her mental map fuzzy. Bilal Mosque was supposed to be around eight blocks up from the dealership, and the dental clinic not far from that. She trudged back to the car dealership, her leg aching, and took a right at the corner this time. But no mosque materialized on the eighth, ninth, or tenth street.

The last time she'd seen the mosque's elegant green dome was when she'd been on the back of her brother Jad's motorcycle, and it was instantly recognizable. Her steps faltered as the old memory came to life, of riding with her good-natured brother as he wove through traffic, going faster at her urging. Heat flared across her cheeks. *I lied to him. Told him that Mama said it was okay for him to take me to the audition.* Nadia had known the moment Rima had shown her the advertisement on the television station's website requesting models her age that her mother would never let her go. So she'd tricked Jad into taking her. She'd then beaten out over a hundred other girls to win the part. Back at home, she'd defiantly told her parents the news, and in the end, her father's good humor had overcome her mother's disapproval. She'd been reprimanded, but they'd let her appear in the television commercial.

The memory sent a thrill through her heart, but the golden spark quickly turned to ash. *What use is it now? To have been chosen to smile in front of a camera, holding a big box of powdered milk?* She'd been recognized on the streets for a few months after the commercial had run, and become a celebrity at school, with girls vying to sit next to her at lunch. But the fame had faded, like the fleeting blossoms of the apricot trees that bloomed in the garden of her grandparents' country house. *And now? Now it doesn't matter at all.* Shoving aside the bittersweet thoughts, Nadia realized she had to retrace her steps, and fast. She bit her lip, staring up at the full moon glowing behind the clouds. Her mother and aunts had probably met up with the men, and she prayed they hadn't left.

Start back at the car dealership, she thought, turning back around. *Maybe I have to go another direction this time.* She ran, passing a tire and part of a carburetor crumbled on the street. She jogged on while lecturing herself that she should have paid more attention when her mother drove her to the dentist. *I am the harebrained hamster that Razan always accuses me of being,* she thought, jaw clenched. But after nearly an hour of searching, there was no mosque anywhere. A sob caught in her throat, threatening to suffocate her. If she couldn't find the mosque, there was no way to figure out how to reach Dr. Asbahi's clinic.

The heady mixture of anger and adrenaline that had driven her this far evaporated. She spotted a man scurrying up the street across from her. Throat parched, she called out to him, to ask how to find her way, but he hurried on, ignoring her. Exhausted, she hobbled toward the tattered awning of what used to be a restaurant and leaned against the front wall. The remaining building had been reduced to rubble, a crushed mess of tables and chairs, utensils, pans, broken plates, and hints of spilled flour and smashed spice bottles. Along the window fluttered faded pictures from the menu; creamy *hummus* with pita bread; lemony *fattoush* salad; kabobs cooked with sour cherries; *lahm bi ajeen*, a pizza with lamb; and one of her favorites, juicy links of *sujuk*, spicy sausages, and garlicky potatoes. A violent rumble protested from her stomach.

Her last meal had been a thin rice porridge she'd helped Nana prepare the night before. It had been the last of the rice, a few bouillon cubes, and spices. All the other scraps of food had been packed away for their trip before they left.

She rested her head against the surprisingly intact window, letting the tears run down her face. *Left. They all left me, even Mishmish. How could they?*

As she wallowed in self-pity, a voice echoed from her memory, from when they'd been fleeing early that morning: *I don't believe it—she is alive. . . . Find her!*

Nana. Her grandmother hadn't believed she was dead. She'd wanted to stay and look for her. Nadia's heart rate quickened. Nana. Always her confidant, the one who loved watching old movies and soaps as much as she did, and the one who'd always told her she should reach for the stars and be who she wanted to be . . . *but with a bit more decorum and manners*. Nadia smiled. Nana would be at the clinic, forcing them to at least wait through the night for her.

Hope burned through the haze of hunger and exhaustion. She stared out over the street and was startled to see that the wind had picked up, dragging a trail of tattered newspaper and clanking soda cans. Then, all of a sudden, she could smell it—a familiar sweet, pungent scent. *Rain.* A memory came tumbling back, of standing with her father on the balcony, laughing as a rainstorm sprinkled their upturned faces. She'd asked him about the smell that mysteriously appeared when it was about to rain, and he'd been more than happy to talk about his favorite subject: chemistry. The unique odor came from a type of oxygen—ozone, he'd called it, from the Greek word meaning "smelling."

You need to find shelter, warned a voice inside her head as she pushed away the memory. *You're already lost—it's dark . . . dangerous. . . . Once the rain stops, find someone to give you directions to the clinic.*

A crack of lightning illuminated the sky, followed seconds later by the crash of thunder. Nadia scurried from under the awning, her bag heavy against her back. Without sparing her even a minute to find cover, the first daggers of icy rain lashed against her face.

Blindly she ran down the street, scanning desperately for a place to hide. The street was deserted. She skipped the first storefront, which was blocked by a rolling metal gate, and collapsed against the door to a butcher shop. But the handle wouldn't budge. *Locked.* She scurried to the next, a tailor. *Also locked.* The windows were broken, but she couldn't crawl through without getting cut. As rain soaked through her coat, she crashed against the next door, desperately twisting the handle. *Locked.* With a cry of fury, she shoved hard with her shoulder. And to her surprise, it swung inward.

Nadia careened inside, toppling to the dusty floor. She lay there a second, teeth chattering from the cold, listening. But besides the drum of rain, it was silent. She opened her bag and rooted around for her flashlight and then stood. Everyone in her family had packed a flashlight; they had hoarded batteries for the past few months. Deep gashes in the wooden frame hinted that the door had been pried open. It hung loose, the lock useless. With trembling, mittened fingers she pushed it closed, hoping to find something to wedge it shut. Her flashlight revealed counters running along both sides of the long, rectangular room. Beyond them rose narrow shelves, mostly bare. A few bottles and packets lay scattered. The arc of light moved to the back wall, pinned with advertisements for blood pressure medicine, lipsticks, eye drops, and pills to stop flatulence.

It's a pharmacy, she thought, cautiously walking toward a set of torn maroon curtains hanging from the wall at the back. She pushed aside the heavy fabric and found a small office, ransacked and empty. All that remained was a wooden desk, a rickety metal chair, and stacks of files, most of them strewn across the floor. With a relieved sigh, Nadia grabbed a few thick files and returned to the door to wedge them under the gap. Someone could push it open, but it was the best she could do. For now, she had to stay as dry and warm as possible. October nights in Aleppo could turn brutally cold and she had none of the blankets her aunts had been carrying. Getting sick now would be a disaster.

Back inside the office, she slipped off her coat and lay it across the desk to dry out as best it could. She wished she could start a fire but she didn't have any matches. Her gaze fell on the curtains and she wrenched them from the wall. Wrapping them around her shivering body, she crawled under the desk and curled up like a caterpillar forming a cocoon, listening to the patter of rain against the window. As warmth seeped into her weary muscles, her eyelids grew heavy. *Don't go to sleep!* She pinched her arm as the beam from the flashlight flickered. Grudgingly, she turned it off, not wanting to waste the batteries. As the comforting golden glow disappeared, it transformed the deep maroon of the curtain a blood red.

Chapter Seven

January 15, 2011

"It's been a month since Mohamed Bouazizi, the disgruntled vegetable vendor from Tunisia, lit himself on fire and died," reported Sara at Syria One News, her bright red lips pronouncing each word with care. Except for her youngest cousins, everyone in Nadia's family sat glued to the television, drapes pulled tight.

Nadia lounged in the back, listening with half an ear, applying another coat of Purple Passion polish to her nails and waiting patiently for everyone to leave so she could watch *Arab Idol*. But she was feeling pretty magnanimous, since the milk commercial she'd starred in had just run for the first time earlier that day. Over a dozen calls from her friends had come in, telling her how fabulous she'd been, so she didn't want to make a fuss, especially since Jiddo looked particularly worried about what the newscaster was reporting.

"We now have breaking news to report," said Sara, staring intently into the camera, eyes narrowed. "The president of Tunisia, Ben Ali, unable to manage the discord in his country, has stepped down after twenty-three years of rule and fled to Saudi Arabia."

Nadia looked up. *The president ran away to Saudi Arabia?* She looked at her father, but he didn't look particularly shocked, nor did the other grown-ups.

She heard Ammo Zayn laugh without humor. "Discord. She calls it *discord*, like they had a disagreement over what to serve for dinner!"

"Well, she's not going to tell us what we already know," said Nadia's mother. "Now that everyone can watch foreign satellite channels like Al Jazeera, they can't hide the truth of what's really happening outside Syria."

Her father took her mother's hand and squeezed it. "Ben Ali had no choice," he said. "After all the demonstrations demanding political and economic reforms, and with over a dozen Tunisians dead, he never kept his promise to hold elections, or make concrete changes."

"Yup," said Ammo Hadi with a humorless smile.

"He was pretty much run out of town like a dog with his tail between his legs."

"Careful what you say," snapped Jiddo. He was pale and his hands shook when he reached for his tea. Nana helped him, worry in her eyes as her gaze met Nadia's. Her grandfather had had a stroke a week after her birthday party, and seemed to grow weaker by the day. Nadia grabbed a box of tissues and took it to her grandparents. Jiddo patted her cheek with a tired smile.

"It's not just Al Jazeera," said Jad, now eighteen and a member of the adult club. "People are getting their news from the Internet, from sites like Facebook and Twitter."

"What book and what's that?" asked Jiddo, looking confused.

"Jiddo." Jad smiled, two dimples appearing on his handsome cheeks. "They're places on the computer where people share news. That's how I knew about the clashes taking place in Jordan, Algeria, and Oman after what really happened to Bouazizi. Anyone can post pictures and videos of what's happening, and connect with other people to organize demonstrations."

"I'm sure the Assad regime is not happy about this," prophesized Ammo Zayn, his voice low.

Nadia shivered, *Arab Idol* forgotten for the moment.

Soon after Ben Ali fled Tunisia, Egyptians took to the streets and camped out on Tahrir Square in the heart of Cairo. Within days their president, Hosni Mubarak, tumbled from his dictatorship. Then came Yemen, Bahrain, Morocco, and Libya. Ammo Ramzi, married to Khala Lina, brought back newspapers from a business trip to London, and as Nadia sat at the dining room table looking for the fashion section, she noted similar headlines emblazoned across the front pages: ARAB SPRING TAKES ROOT IN THE MIDDLE EAST.

That's what it was being called in the West: the Arab Spring—uprisings across the Middle East, challenging corrupt authoritarian regimes. Intrigued by the adults' worried, hushed conversations, Nadia ran a search on the Internet using Jad's laptop and found a definition of "authoritarian."

Not fully getting what it meant, she lugged the computer to her father, who was in his office. A tad annoyed to be pulled away from a pile of contracts he was examining, he sighed, running a hand over his balding head. At first, Nadia thought he would tell her not to worry about such things, but he surprised her by explaining that an authoritarian regime was a ruler or government that held complete power over the lives of its people, and that the people were not free to choose their leader, or the rules that governed their country. When he noticed the computer screen, his lips tightened.

"These are uneasy times," he said, voice gruff. "A search like this might be noticed by *someone*. . . . Erase your search history and *never* do a search like this again. If you have questions, come to me."

For once, Nadia didn't argue. She was surprised by the fear in his eyes, their color a shade darker blue than hers. *Someone*. In her gut she knew what he meant. All Syrians did. Their president, Bashar al-Assad, was the son of the country's previous president, Hafez al-Assad, who'd come to power in a military coup in 1970. In school she had learned that the Assad family were their saviors and guardians, the ones who built modern Syria and maintained peace and prosperity. It was drilled into her that only they could keep the religious and ethnic groups from fighting one another. But on the streets, in the shops, mosques, churches, salons, and universities, the *mukhabarat* and their informants were everywhere, listening and reporting back what they learned, making people who disagreed or dissented with the Assad regime disappear into the night. . . . *They fit the definition of "authoritarian regime": a ruler or government willing to do anything to keep their power,* thought Nadia with a sinking feeling in her stomach.

Chapter Eight

October 10, 2013 4:56 a.m.

For the third time in the past twenty-four hours, Nadia awoke with a start, muscles sore, brain befuddled, not quite certain where she was. Then it all came rushing back. She sat up, head thumping the underside of the desk. Grimacing in pain, she threw off the heavy curtains and stuck her head out from beneath the desk. Silence greeted her ears. The rain had stopped, and the window was still a small dark square. Relief that she hadn't slept away the night evaporated after she squinted down at her watch. Dawn was barely an hour away. She crawled out, pulled on her damp coat, and grabbed her bags. As she moved toward the doorway, a sharp bang echoed at the front of the store, followed by a slow creak.

Heart in her throat, Nadia retreated beneath the desk, making herself as small as possible. A dozen possibilities of who it could be raced through her mind: Syrian army troops, *mukhabarat*, or worse, *shabiha*. . . . Her father's whispered conversations tumbled through her mind, of what the *shabiha* did to people they thought were traitors. Or it could be one of the rebel groups. If that was the case, she could tell them that her father was one of them—maybe they would help her.

At first she didn't see the small glowing lights, not until they appeared at the office door. They were low to the ground . . . coming straight for her. . . . *What on earth* . . . The lights narrowed and picked up speed while Nadia flattened herself against the back of the desk. Muffling a cry, she tensed as a furry object leapt into her chest and buried its cold nose in her neck. Mishmish! Nadia released a hot rush of air as purring filled her ears. "You silly, silly cat," she whispered hoarsely, her face sinking into his damp pelt. Joy quickly evaporated as footsteps came through the doorway and into the pharmacy.

We have to get out of here, Nadia thought.

She slithered out from beneath the desk, set Mishmish on the floor, and tried to open the window. It was sealed shut, probably to keep thieves out. In growing panic, she spun around, looking for another escape route. *Nothing.*

Calm down! she told herself. *Take a deep breath. Think. . . .*

Whoever was out there didn't know she was back here. Maybe, just maybe, she could make a run for it. She tucked Mishmish inside his burlap bag, then got back on her hands and knees and crawled toward the doorway. Flattened against the edge, she paused, shoulders tense, trying to hear what was going on. Someone snorted, then came the clatter of boots. Nadia tried to count—there seemed to be an awful lot of feet out there.

"Now, now, don't be upset, my dear," came a calm, gravelly voice. An irritated snort came in response. "I just need to stop here for a bit. We'll find a more comfortable spot after our meeting with Alaa."

Nadia frowned. This sure didn't sound like hardened soldiers, or rebels. She heard the front door shut with a thud, which alarmed her. A few seconds later, soft light spilled in through the doorway that led to the back office where she hid. Nadia gingerly peeked around the corner, and her eyes widened. In the middle of the pharmacy stood a slight man in loose woolen pantaloons and a navy vest, a *taqiyah* (skull cap) covering his cropped white hair. With his back to her, he leaned over to inspect the contents of the shelves. Past him, near the door, stood a sturdy, dun-colored donkey. Nadia stared at the stout, long-eared beast, who eyed the man balefully and snorted again.

"Not exactly what I need, but there are some useful things left," muttered the man, crouching down to inspect the floor. He picked up bottles and packages and stacked them along the counter, then searched the crevices along the floorboard.

A surge of relief flooded through Nadia as she eyed the old man. She knew better than to assume he was no threat, but at least he didn't look like a soldier or cold-blooded assassin. She calculated the distance to the door, which unfortunately had a donkey blocking it. But if she ran for it, she could make it. The man had crossed to the other side of the store and slipped behind the counter to scrutinize a line of dusty bottles on the top shelf.

Nadia kneaded her thigh, then her calves, working out the tightness. Somehow she just had to get around that donkey and through the door. With a deep breath, she gave Mishmish a pat and stepped through the office door at a dead run. Eyes locked on the animal, she made a snap judgment. She ducked and went under its stubby legs, inhaling a wet, musky scent as she reached the door on the other side. She grabbed the handle and pulled, just as the ornery donkey backed up with a huff. The door jammed, arrested by the animal's hairy backside. There was no way to slip out.

Trembling, Nadia turned and saw the old man still standing on the other side of the counter, looking at her with a startled expression on his bearded face.

"Hello, my dear," he said calmly, as if he were meeting her in her grandparents' living room for a dinner party. "It appears you are in quite a rush." His bright amber eyes glinted through silver spectacles.

Nadia swallowed, her tongue thick and dry in her mouth. "Um . . . yes," she said, the words popping out of her mouth. "I'm really in a hurry to get somewhere."

"I see," said the man. "Well, if you'd like, Jamila can move, and you can open the door and proceed."

"Yes, that would be very helpful," said Nadia,

shifting the bags on her shoulder. Mishmish chose that moment to pop out his head and yowl.

The donkey's ears perked up and she turned her head toward Nadia so that the two animals' noses could touch.

"I see that you have found your cat," said the man. "He was following us all evening and stopped at this store as we made our way through the rain. He would not budge until I opened the door for him."

"I thought I had lost him," said Nadia, giving Mishmish a scratch under his chin as a jumble of emotions bubbled within her. "Thank you for helping him find me."

"*Alhamdulillah*, thanks to *Allah*, you both found each other again," said the man, raising the flashlight he had toward Nadia. "It looks like you have quite a cut on your forehead." He passed her one of the small tubes he'd collected. "You should apply some of this, it will keep away infection."

Nadia took the antibiotic cream with a shaking hand. The kindness in his words penetrated deep in her heart, and, without warning, tears rolled down her cheeks. "Everything has all gone so wrong," she sniffed. An avalanche of words tumbled from her mouth, telling him all that had happened, ending with: "Do you have a mobile phone?"

"No, my dear," said the man, shaking his head. "I do not care for such newfangled things."

"Do you know where Asbahi Clinic is located?" she asked, hoping at least for directions.

"Yes, I do," said the man.

"Can you tell me how to get there?" asked Nadia, hope renewed.

"This area has become very dangerous with the approaching battle," said the man. "It is not safe for a girl to be out alone."

"Yes, I know about the battle, my father told me," said Nadia. "But I have to go. . . . I'm already late, and if I don't reach my family, they'll think I'm dead and leave for Turkey without me."

The man took a deep breath, his lips pursed as if pondering something. "I will take you there," he said finally.

"You will?" squeaked Nadia, surprised.

"Yes," he said. "It's only a half an hour walk from here, if things go smoothly."

Nadia paused, staring at the frail old man, a moment

of uncertainty flaring as she wondered if it was wise to go with a stranger. "Okay, thank you," she finally said, realizing that at this moment she had no other choice.

The man sighed. "All right. Let me collect some things and we shall be on our way."

Chapter Nine

October 10, 2013   6:09 a.m.

Nadia stood at the pharmacy door, watching the old man efficiently harness Jamila to a small four-wheeled cart parked on the street, a tarp covering its top. He leaned down to refasten the cloth wrapping on the donkey's hooves.

"Why are you doing that?"

"To muffle her footsteps," he replied. "It is wise to be stealthy on the roads these days."

Nadia nodded. Like a pesky splinter, doubt dug into her skin as Khala Lina's lecture to all the kids not to play outside came back to her—during desperate times, people did bad things to one another, and you needed to be careful of strangers. *Who is this man, really?* she thought. *Should I trust him?*

"Before we reach the clinic, I need to run a small errand," he said, checking a silver compass. "It won't take long," he added, slipping the instrument into his pocket. "It's on the way to the clinic."

Fingers clinging to the doorframe, familiar whispers rang in her mind. *Don't go outside. It's safer here.* Nadia stared down at the ground. "Stop it," she hissed, pulling her woolen cap over her ears.

"Are you all right?" asked the old man.

"I . . . ," began Nadia, "I don't like being outside."

The man nodded. "Yes, it's difficult for many. Living under the fear of being bombed and hearing mortar and gunfire for so long can have a terrible effect on the body and the mind."

She nodded, tongue-tied as she battled both her fear of being outside and the uncertainty of trusting a man she'd just met. The man lifted a corner of the tarp and rooted around in his cart. "Here," he said, handing her a dark blue visor with what looked to be flaps on both sides. "Wear this, pulled low over your eyes. Stay beside me and keep your eyes focused in front of you."

Nadia took the hat, again surprised by his kindness. She realized that she had to trust him, at a least a little, if she was going to find her family. Once he dropped her off at the clinic, he'd be gone. She snugly fit the visor over her father's olive-green cap and pushed away from the door. The hat made it so she could see only in front of her. She found it surprisingly calming. Relieved, she took a deep, ragged breath. The air, usually a mix of gunpowder, smoke, concrete dust, and rotting garbage, smelled fresh, cleansed by the rains. She took a quick peek at the sky and spotted a line of pinkish-yellow light licking the eastern edge of the city. Silence pressed against them from all sides, as if they were the only inhabitants of the city. But soon the chirp of birds trilled through the air, welcoming dawn.

"We needed this rain years ago," muttered the old man as he took off down the street.

Nadia had heard similar things from her father. *What did he call it? Climate change. Yes, that's it.* He'd explained how burning fossil fuels like oil and coal was warming up the earth. In Syria, it had triggered a seven-year drought, turning rich farmland into dust. Their livelihoods gone, farmers flooded into the cities. Driven to despair, their voices had merged with others in the rising tide against the government.

"If we are to be traveling companions," said the man, "we should at least know one another's name, don't you think? I am old Mazen—you can call me old Ammo Mazen."

Nadia hesitated, glancing at the man's tanned, wrinkled features. There was no guile in his eyes, just open curiosity. She decided to go with her gut and blurted out, "My name is Nadia. Nadia Jandali."

"Jandali?" asked the man, cocking his head. "Jandali . . . Jandali . . . Jandali . . . ," he repeated as if mentally thumbing through a dusty set of files in his head. "Is that the same Jandali family that runs Jandali Chemical Industries?"

"Yes," said Nadia, smiling with pride. "My grandfather started the business, but my father and uncles help him run it." *Or used to run it,* she thought with a sigh, eyeing Ammo Mazen's ragged leather shoes, shabby clothes, and work-worn hands. She wondered what his story was.

"So tell me where in Aleppo you are from," he asked, turning northeast toward the widening arc of light.

But before she could answer, they heard the screech of tires from up the road. Ammo Mazen stiffened. "Come," he urged, pulling Jamila into what appeared to be the remains of a butcher shop. Its front metal shutters were gone, the back wall partially caved in, but it provided enough cover to be hidden from the street. Nadia darted in, alongside the cart, spotting the metal hooks still hanging from the ceiling. "Quiet, girl," Ammo Mazen whispered into Jamila's ear. He pointed for Nadia to hide behind the counter. As she ducked down, she caught sight of a black Mercedes cruising by, tinted windows rolled up. *Mukhabarat.*

Ten minutes later, they emerged from their hiding spot. "No good messing with those boys," said Ammo Mazen. "So now, what did I ask you? Oh yes, where in Aleppo are you from?"

"Our home was past the stadium, on the western edge of Salaheddine." A lump rose in her throat as images of their destroyed apartment building came back.

"Ah, Salaheddine. That part of the city has borne the mother of all battles since the war began," said Ammo Mazen, shaking his head sadly.

Nadia nodded, pushing back memories of a hot evening in July, more than a year ago, when gunfire had broken out a few miles from their home, triggering the battle for Aleppo.

"What a shame it all is," said Ammo Mazen. "Salaheddine would be turning over in his grave."

"Huh?" mumbled Nadia, not really paying attention as bitter thoughts raced through her head of the day when life as she had known it had changed forever.

"Don't they teach you anything in school these days?" he asked with a smile as he guided Jamila around a burned-out shell of a bus. "Your neighborhood was named after the great Kurdish warrior who united the lands from North Africa to Syria. He drove European crusaders from the holy city of Jerusalem and founded the Ayyubid dynasty."

"I know who he is," muttered Nadia, cheeks red. Actually, she and Nana, while working in the kitchen as they usually did, had watched *al-Nasir Salaheddine al-Ayyubi*, a soap opera about Salaheddine. It was a swashbuckling adventure, filled with battles, intrigues, great one-liners, and beautiful heroines, who always managed to look perfectly made-up even in the middle of a battle scene.

"I'm glad to hear it." Ammo Mazen smiled, a twinkle in his eye. "He was quite a man, that Salaheddine."

Nadia nodded. Even though she didn't much care about dead historical figures, or living ones either, he had a point. Salaheddine had been respected, even by his enemies, for his fairness in battle. The guy who'd played him in the show had been gorgeous, with his long dark hair and chocolate-brown eyes. He hadn't been the best actor, but he'd looked impressive enough for the part, especially when he'd taken Jerusalem and spared the lives of all the Christians and Jews in the city.

"Where are you from?" she asked tentatively, hoping to get a hint of who she was traveling with.

"I grew up in a small village in the mountains," he said, a faraway look in his eyes. "My family had citrus orchards, but the life of growing oranges was not for me. So I went to the sea and became a fisherman, then came back to shore, called by the love of books, especially old books that needed repair and rebinding. So a book repairer I became. I found that it is only by being a little lost that you stumble upon the path that is meant for you."

"Oh," Nadia said, thinking his life sounded pretty interesting.

They walked past the car dealership Nadia had criss-crossed the night before, and turned left on the tenth corner, not the eighth or ninth. Nadia caught sight of a torn poster she'd missed the night before and stumbled to a stop, seething with a sudden burst of rage. Without even realizing what she was doing, she took aim and spat, hitting the narrow, weak-chinned face, a tooth-brush mustache stretched across his upper lip. Beneath Bashar al-Assad's portrait was written THE LEADER FOREVER, but someone had crossed out *forever* and put *never*.

"Come," said Ammo Mazen gently. "There's nothing for you there."

"He's a killer," she hissed, eyebrows knitted over stormy eyes.

"Yes, he is," he said softly. "In over seventy years of life, I've realized that every person's destiny leads them on a tumultuous journey. And if given bountiful blessings, how they choose to use them determines their humanity."

Nadia looked at him, irritated at his riddle.

"The lot of the Alawites has not always been so enviable," he said, referring to the religious group to which the Assad family and the ruling party belonged.

Nadia bristled. "They are evil and hateful," she hissed.

"Yes, today their actions are," said Ammo Mazen. "But long ago, under Ottoman rule, they were abused and reviled. Alawite women and children were sold into slavery."

Nadia frowned. She'd never heard that before.

"When Hafez came to power, he brought order to a country fractured by years of turmoil, and promised security for minorities. He modernized, built Syria's infrastructure, and instituted educational reform."

"While oppressing the majority of the population," said Nadia. Ten percent of Syrians were Christian; seventy percent followed the Sunni branch of Islam, like her family; and the remainder were Shia. And within the Shia branch existed sects like the Alawites.

"Yes," said Ammo Mazen. "Once Alawites were oppressed, but when they took power, they used it to oppress others."

Nadia snorted. Alawites dominated most of the influential positions in the government and army, including the *mukhabarat* and much of the *shabiha*. It was a known fact that those close to the Assad family had a monopoly on lucrative businesses. Because of Alawite domination, cars and mobile phones were more expensive in Syria than in England. Her cheeks reddened with heat as she acknowledged that Sunni businessmen, like her grandfather, had worked with the Alawite government to secure their own financial success. It was a devilish deal, she thought, an uneasy truce orchestrated by President Hafez al-Assad—staged economic progress and stability in exchange for military rule and dictatorship.

As the sun rose in the distance, Nadia calculated that it had been over twenty-four hours since the *barmeela* had rained down on her home and her family. *What if they're gone?* she wondered. *They probably think I'm dead, so why would they wait for me?* She opened the burlap bag for a soothing rub under Mishmish's chin, but before she could get a good grip, he shot out from the sack and ran past a burned-out pizza shop into an alley.

"Hey!" cried Nadia, ready to run after him.

"Don't worry," said Ammo Mazen with a weary smile. "I know where he is."

Nadia frowned. *Is he clairvoyant or something?* She bit her tongue and followed the cart. At the far end of the alley, the hazy blue of early morning met the edge of a cobblestone square. A red ambulance was parked at the corner. As they emerged from the alley, her jaw dropped open. A writhing mass of black, gray, white, and orange fur surrounded a man. He carried a heavy plastic bag and tossed out bits of meat. Mishmish cut through the mass of cats, swatted away a scrawny tabby, and snatched a morsel from the man's hand.

"*Salaam*, Alaa," Ammo Mazen called out.

"*Walaikum assalaam*, uncle," replied the disheveled, wiry young man, a hint of relief in his voice as he hurried over. "Boy, am I glad you made it. I was worried you'd been held up at some checkpoint."

"When I got the note that you'd tracked down the item, no force was going to hold me back." Ammo Mazen smiled as he brought Jamila to a halt beside the ambulance.

"I got lucky," said Alaa. "I found the fellow easily enough, though I had to twist his arm to hand it over."

"Thankfully, it worked out," said Ammo Mazen, moving to the back of the cart.

Alaa held out the bag toward Nadia. "Do you mind?"

Repulsed by the bloodstains and rotten smell, she grudgingly took it. Within seconds the cats scrambled toward her, standing on their hind legs, digging claws into her jeans, begging. She took out bits of gristly, grayish meat and started tossing them out while watching the men from the corner of her eye. Alaa slipped into the back of his ambulance and emerged with a package wrapped in brown paper. Nadia caught an address scrawled in black ink across the top as he handed it to the old man.

Ammo Mazen hid the package in the back of his cart and slipped Alaa a thick wad of bills. "I hope this will help your family. I know times are tough."

"They're tough for everyone," said Alaa. "I fear this war is going to get worse. It's getting too difficult for me to come out to feed the cats."

"Do you come every day?" Nadia couldn't help but ask as she gave Mishmish a meaty chunk.

"No," laughed Alaa as Nadia handed the bag back to him. "I'm lucky if I can do it once a week. Meat is getting harder and harder to find."

"Alaa," said Ammo Mazen, "the other thing . . . were you able to find any?"

Alaa's face drooped. "I'm afraid not, uncle. And believe me, I looked. Two other clinics and a hospital were bombed last week, and we have few places to take patients and get our hands on medications."

"I understand," sighed Ammo Mazen, folding Jamila's reins in his hands.

"Oh," added Alaa, a worried look on his face, "I heard Sulaiman is looking for you."

"Sulaiman? Are you sure?" asked Ammo Mazen, his face inscrutable.

Alaa nodded. "It was something to do with the information you were collecting for him. He needs it."

"Thank you for telling me," said Ammo Mazen. "Now, keep yourself safe and your cats well fed, for there is great reward in caring for all of *Allah*'s creatures."

"I will, uncle," said Alaa, enveloping the old man in a hug and kissing his cheeks. "I pray that you keep well," Alaa added, his eyes troubled as he watched them leave.

Chapter Ten

October 10, 2013   7:31 a.m.

The main road was still eerily quiet. Eyes forward, Nadia walked beside the cart, mind filled with images of a joyous reunion with her family.

"You there, stop!" hollered an authoritative voice, making Nadia stumble.

"Gentle, now," whispered Ammo Mazen as he placed his hand on Jamila's neck to slow her down.

A group of masked figures emerged from a side street up ahead: a dozen or so troops, marching in line, wearing heavy military fatigues and wielding machine guns.

Nadia looked for a place to hide, but Ammo Mazen grabbed her arm. "No sudden movements, child," he whispered.

"Stop and hold up your hands," ordered the leader, voice muffled behind the mask. "You should not be out. We have word that the Syrian army is gathering at the western edge of the district and will be making a push soon."

Nadia relaxed. But only a little. They were a rebel group.

"Thank you for your concern," said Ammo Mazen. "We are on our way to safety now."

"What do you have under there?" asked a tall soldier, prodding the canvas with the muzzle of a rifle.

Nadia scooted behind Ammo Mazen, keeping her eyes downcast as the group encircled them. *That's strange,* she thought with a frown. The soldier doing all the talking had remarkably small feet. Encased in pink tennis shoes.

"Nothing too interesting, just an old man's odds and ends," chuckled Ammo Mazen. He gently lifted up the canvas. Beneath the protective layer of thick plastic lay an assortment of neatly packed items: a basket of wood, metal tools, and folded clothes. Stacked on one side lay a pile of books, mostly old, the leather bindings cracked, paper faded.

"Yes, bread would be far more useful," grumbled the tall soldier.

They tensed as Ammo Mazen slowly reached for a burlap sack near the basket of wood. From the corner of her eye Nadia saw him pull out a box, its golden cover glinting in the sun.

"Oh!" gasped one of the soldiers.

Nadia read the dark brown lettering on the box. *Ghraoui.* She stared at Ammo Mazen in surprise. Ghraoui was the most expensive chocolatier in Syria, and on special occasions her father had brought a similar box home for her mother or Nana.

"I believe a taste of sweetness will serve you well as you head for the front line," said Ammo Mazen, breaking open the seal.

"Thank you, Ammo," said the soldier nearest him, taking a dark chocolate truffle, which Nadia recalled was filled with pistachio paste.

As the box was passed around, the others lifted up their masks.

Nadia stood with her mouth hanging open for the second time. They were all women.

"Well, I'm glad we ran into you," said Ammo Mazen, pulling the tarp back in place. "We need to get to the eastern edge of the district. Is it safe?"

"Where are you going?" asked the one in pink tennis shoes. She had broad, angular features and full lips. Her chin had a scar from a recent injury.

"To Dr. Asbahi's clinic on Saif al-Dawla Street," said Ammo Mazen.

"You want to go to a dentist?" asked one of the women, eyebrow raised.

"Hey, you know the joke about dentists, right?" giggled another.

"No, tell us," replied the tall one with a grin.

"Well, it's the only safe place in Syria to open your mouth!"

The women roared in laughter, and even Nadia cracked a smile. She'd heard the joke before. It played on the fear that you had to keep your mouth shut lest something popped out that got you in trouble with the *mukhabarat*. The box of chocolates came her way and she took one of her favorites, a rich buttery caramel bathed in milk chocolate. She popped it into her mouth, her first morsel of food in over twenty-four hours. She sighed as the chocolate melted on her tongue.

"We passed the clinic on our morning rounds yesterday around noon," said a rosy-cheeked girl who looked like she should have been on her way to university, not in a war zone.

"Were you there yesterday?" asked Nadia, nearly choking on the chocolate. "Did you see a group of women and children there?"

The women looked at each other and shrugged. "No," said the woman in pink shoes. "We didn't see anyone there."

Maybe her aunts and mother were late getting to the clinic. *They might still be there.*

"We can walk with you there," said the tall one. "Some of us will be passing by on our way to the field hospital."

The group split up, half the women marching off to assemble on the front line while the rest accompanied them.

"What have you heard of the approaching battle?" Ammo Mazen asked the fresh-faced girl, whose name they'd learned was Maria.

"The news is not good, Ammo," said Maria, her brow furrowed. "Ever since the Syrian army began Operation Northern Storm this summer, trying to recapture territory in and around Aleppo, things have been getting worse. And now with telecommunications down, it's hard to get word of what is actually happening around the city. Before, we could get news from bloggers and undercover journalists from their Facebook posts and tweets."

"Yes, with Hezbollah fighters flooding in from Lebanon to support the president, there must be terrible pressure on you," murmured Ammo Mazen.

Maria nodded, tight-lipped. "This is our fight—the Syrian people against heartless Assad, who is now bringing in his foreign cronies to kill us."

Nadia stared at her, awed by her strength and bravery.

The tall one walking beside Nadia added, "Last week sixteen of our brothers were killed in an ambush while trying to slip into Salaheddine."

"Sixteen? That's terrible," said Ammo Mazen, eyes troubled.

"There is trouble in the air. We can feel it," said Maria, licking the last of the chocolate from her fingers.

"What rebel group are you part of?" Nadia couldn't help but ask.

"We are our own group," said the tall girl proudly.

"We named ourselves the Mother Aisha battalion, after the Prophet Mohammad's wife Aisha."

"Yes," added Maria. "After all, Aisha led troops into battle and served as consultant to the Prophet's followers in his absence."

"Yes, a noble name," said Ammo Mazen, nodding.

"If we don't defend ourselves and our families, who will?" added Maria with a mixture of pride and sadness.

One of the other women let out a tired sigh. Nadia glimpsed that she was adjusting the contents of her bag. A set of knitting needles and skeins of grass-green yarn poked out. When she saw Nadia looking, she gave her a weary smile. "After the war I just want things to return to how they were," she said.

Nadia nodded wholeheartedly, willing to do just about anything to go back to how things were. *But how were they exactly?* she wondered. They would still have lived under the axe of Assad rule, ready to fall at any time.

"Once we put Assad in the ground, you can," said her companion, thumping her on the back.

But Nadia's mind had wandered from the conversation. They had turned onto Saif al-Dawla Street and her eyes desperately sought their destination. The clinic was a few blocks down.

Maria looked at her watch. "We must leave you here. Go quickly and hide yourselves. Barricade the windows and doors," she advised.

The women pulled down their masks.

"Thank you for your assistance, and may *Allah* protect you," said Ammo Mazen. The women slipped into an alley and disappeared. Nadia stared after them, already missing their protection. "Come, we must hurry. I do not like this mention of trouble brewing, and we need to find shelter for the day," said Ammo Mazen.

Nadia hurried, her eyes on the sign for Asbahi's dental clinic at the end of the street.

Chapter Eleven

October 10, 2013 9:37 a.m.

Nadia grabbed the metal handle and pulled. *Please. Please be here.* She dropped her packs on the dusty waiting room floor, sending Mishmish tumbling to the ground. Annoyed, he sat, tail swishing from side to side, watching Nadia run from one side of the room to the other, past overturned waiting room chairs, calling out, "Mama, are you here?" She paused to glance anxiously at Ammo Mazen as he entered.

"Nana? Khala Lina?" she added, then hurried toward the door behind the receptionist's black lacquered desk, where the examining rooms were located. A memory came back from her visit, when she'd had to have a baby tooth pulled. The pain she'd felt then was nothing compared to the agony flooding through her as she encountered one empty room after another. She ran back into the waiting room, hoping to find stairs leading to second-floor offices. Maybe they were there.

"Stop, my child," Ammo Mazen said, his voice forceful.

She froze, watching him point toward a message scrawled across the white walls with slashes of dark blue ink, the letters distinctly from her mother's elegant hand.

> *Nadia, my love, we pray that you are safe and find this message. We sent Malik back to the house to find you, as we hoped that you'd survived the bombing. When he returned with news that there was no trace of you, we knew that you had survived. We waited for a day, hoping you would find your way to us. But with news of another battle approaching, we had no choice but to leave. Nadia, read this carefully: Make your way along the same route we journeyed on our way to Kharab Shams, our old picnic spot. The Turkish border is not far from there. Your father will wait for you at Oncupinar border crossing, which faces Bab al-Salama on the Syrian side. Darling, may* Allah *protect you and keep you safe.*

Nadia stood staring at the letters for what seemed like an hour, wondering if she and Malik had crossed paths, before Ammo Mazen's gentle voice broke her from her stupor. "Child, they are gone."

"They left me!" she howled, her body triggered into action. Ammo Mazen stood back, allowing her space. "How could they do that. *Again?*" She paced, glaring at the message. She lunged at a wooden chair and threw it against the wall, where it shattered with a satisfactory *crack*. And as quickly as it had blazed, her anger receded, replaced by a shuddering, overwhelming sense of loss. "How could they?" she whispered.

Ammo Mazen shook his head sadly. "I'm certain they waited as long as they could."

"I know that!" Nadia growled, cheeks hot, her anger unmerciful. "I hate them . . . and I hate Assad . . . and this war . . . *everything*. . . ."

Eyes soft, Ammo Mazen nodded. "I understand your anger, but have mercy on them, my child. It must have torn their hearts in half to leave. In these trying times it is easy to be poisoned by anger."

Nadia lowered her gaze, shame bubbling through her. She'd yelled at a poor old man, and all he'd been trying to do was help. "I'm sorry," she whispered, staring out the long line of glass windows. Jamila, she noticed, stood outside, complacently chomping on bits of green foliage budding on nearby bushes.

"We must leave," said Ammo Mazen, staring at the windows with a frown. "It is not safe with so much glass surrounding us." With a firm hand, he guided Nadia from the building and helped her into the back of the cart. "Come, Jamila, we must be swift of foot and find shelter for the day."

Nadia sat on the edge of the cart, her legs dangling from the back, staring dumbly as the dental clinic grew smaller and smaller behind them. She pulled down the visor Ammo Mazen had given her, blocking out the world, and closed her eyes. A dull thud sounded toward the western edge of the Salaheddine district, followed by another. The skin on the back of Nadia's neck prickled with alarm as a wind whipped up, bringing with it a whiff of scorched metal and gunpowder. She shivered and pulled her coat in tighter. Without the cover of clouds, the temperature had fallen, making it a truly cold, wintery day. Nadia stared down at her lap, clutching the burlap bag, perhaps a bit too tightly.

Mishmish growled from inside, sinking his claws into her thigh. "Ouch," she muttered, opening the mouth of the sack. A flash of orange snaked out and positioned itself at the front of the cart, right behind the donkey. Head angled toward the breeze, the cat twitched his nose.

Minutes later they slowed and Nadia looked up. She recognized a line of dress shops she had often visited with her mother and aunts. They were boarded up and empty now. *How could* Allah *have let all this happen?* she thought. *Does he not love us?* She had voiced this thought in front of her mother, who had told her not to use God's name in vain. But it was Nana who'd later come to her and explained that it was okay to be angry. *Allah* loved his people, but sent them hardships to test their faith. Nadia had listened, but deep in her heart she could not reconcile how such cruelty could be love. She sighed, the bruise in her heart a festering wound.

Ammo Mazen turned in to a narrow lane filled with car part dealers and mechanics and stopped at a sturdy concrete building on the left. A thick metal shutter concealed the entrance. He reached into his coat pocket and pulled out a leather loop, filled with a dozen metal keys. *They're skeleton keys,* Nadia realized in wonder. She'd seen tools like that in the movies, used by thieves to pick locks. *Why does he have a set?* She stared at him, once again wondering, *Who is this man?* Combining a few together, he fit them into a large metal lock. She didn't have much time to ponder further because after a few jiggles the lock sprang open with a sharp click. Lifting up the shutter, Ammo Mazen swatted Jamila's rump, sending her inside. Just as quickly, Ammo Mazen locked the gate shut behind them.

Pale light filtered through small windows lining the top of the wall, illuminating the wide, rectangular, mechanics shop. As Jamila came to a stop, Nadia eased off the cart and set Mishmish down. The cat darted between two cars, suspended on raised platforms, the ground beneath stained with years of engine oil. Nadia walked toward the first, a dusty old Toyota, its hood open, innards from its engine lying in a pile. Careful not to trip over the scattered tools, she inspected the second car, its tires gone, driver-side door dented. A door at the back of the shop probably led to an office. Piled high everywhere were car parts, leather seats, carburetors, vinyl cushions, steering wheels, stereos, and dozens of other odds and ends.

Ammo Mazen took off Jamila's harness and gently rubbed her down with a towel. "'Where is the beauty in a donkey?'" he sang softly. "'The stumpy body, long ears? It's the heroic heart, stubbornness, and intellect behind the long-lashed eyes.'"

Nadia eyed the hairy beast with a wrinkled nose. *Beautiful and smart? Really?* Next he removed a burlap sack from beneath the cart, hidden behind one of the wheels, and fixed it over the tired donkey's head. With a happy snort she began chewing.

"What's that?" asked Nadia.

"Barley," replied Ammo Mazen. "Sadly, moth-eaten, moldy barley, but the finest we can find in the city right now."

While Jamila munched, Ammo Mazen handed Nadia an armful of wood from the cart. "Here, put that in the metal grate," he instructed, pointing to a spot opposite the cars. Next, he extracted a leather rucksack from beneath the cart and hung it from a hook.

For once, she dutifully did as asked, noticing that the wood was from the chair she'd smashed at the dentist's office. After she'd laid it in the bin, Ammo Mazen added bits of kindling and soon had a blaze going.

"Come," he said, tossing a few vinyl cushions beside the brazier. "Grab some bedding from the cart and get warm."

Without having to be told twice, Nadia set up a cozy sleeping pallet and collapsed onto a cushion, her thigh sore from all the walking. Meanwhile, Ammo Mazen puttered around the shop, scavenging through the tools and stowing a few in the cart. Wearily Nadia took off her mittens and stared down at the soft skin of her palms. She raised them toward the fire, feeling the heat soak through, the flames reflecting against the shining shade of Dusty Rose. Her breath caught in her throat. The polish on her thumbnail was chipped. Horrified, she opened her pack and pulled out her precious pink case. She unzipped it and took out a bottle of polish remover, a cotton swab, and a nail file. With mechanical precision, she removed the offending chipped polish and filed the round edge. After applying two coats of Dusty Rose, she waved her hand carefully to let it dry, a sense of relief flooding through her.

As she put her supplies away, she caught sight of an

old, cracked bottle of Tangerine Dreams and the reality of what was happening came flooding back: *My old life is gone. . . . My family is gone. . . .* She hugged herself and began to rock, a soothing motion she'd often seen her mother do while holding Yusuf when the tremors from the war became too much. She stared into the fire, the glowing embers bringing a whirlwind of memories.

Chapter Twelve

March 30, 2011

Nadia sat on the couch in her aunt and uncle's quiet apartment, a box of her favorite cinnamon meringue cookies in her lap. Razan was in her room studying for a zoology exam, while the rest of the kids played outside. The grown-ups huddled over tea at her grandparents', having one of their important *discussions* again. Eyes glued to the television, Nadia watched as the last scene of her favorite *musalselat* (soap opera) came to a dramatic conclusion. Set in a Damascus slum, *Birth from the Loins* followed the lives of its residents as they dealt with poverty and corruption. It was the most talked-about show in the country and Nadia couldn't wait to dissect the juicy plot with her friends at school the next day.

Having fibbed that she needed her cousin's help with her algebra homework, she'd come here, since her mother didn't approve of her watching "mindless junk" at home. As she reached for the remote control to flip off the television, familiar patriotic music blared, accompanied by messages of breaking news on the screen. President Assad was about to speak. Usually uninterested, she hesitated. A familiar phrase bubbled up in the back of her mind, an Internet search she'd erased months ago. *Authoritarian regime.* Without realizing it, she sat up, brushing cookie crumbs from her dress, as a familiar chinless face above a tailored English suit appeared on screen.

Tall, with the grace of a scarecrow, President Assad leaned across the podium, toothbrush mustache quivering as he stared into the camera. "Enemies of Syria have infiltrated the country and are spreading lies and promoting violence," he said. Nadia swallowed, the cookie in her mouth tasting like sawdust. "These foreign agents are conspiring to undermine our beloved country's stability, and our national unity." Her breath caught in her throat as she watched him blame *terrorists* for recent clashes in the south, while promising to crack down with "an iron fist." "God willing, we will be victorious," he declared.

He's lying, thought Nadia, her dress clenched in her fist. Foreign agents hadn't brought unrest to Syria. It had begun with a group of boys from Deraa, a city in the southwest of the country, afflicted by drought and economic hardship. A few weeks ago the rambunctious boys had decided to sneak into their school. They'd spray-painted antigovernment graffiti all over the walls. A few were arrested by security forces, beaten, and tortured. In response, courageous people from all walks of life—doctors, students, workers, taxi drivers, cooks, and farmers—united across religious and ethnic lines, took to the streets, and demanded the return of the children. Nadia had seen the videos on Facebook of peaceful demonstrators marching in the dusty streets, chanting, "God, Syria, freedom" and "One, one, one; the Syrian people are one." They carried white flags and banners stating DERAA IS BLEEDING and WHO KILLS HIS PEOPLE IS A TRAITOR. In response, Assad's troops had fired into the crowd, wounding and killing indiscriminately.

Nadia had heard snippets of hushed conversations among her aunts and uncles and knew that discontent in Syria had been simmering for decades, but any disobedience to the regime invited disaster. After her brother had shown the videos to Jiddo, her grandfather had recalled the events of 1982, when Bashar al-Assad's father, Hafez, massacred thousands of Sunni Muslims in the city of Hama. He'd then quelled unrest among the Kurds and the Shiite Druze, who had risen up against him, by killing them, too. When Hafez was buried in his predominantly Alawite village of Qardaha in the northwest mountains, Syrians hoped for reforms from his son, but they did not come. Unlike the massacres of the eighties, which were easily covered up, the killings in Deraa were visible to the world, across hundreds of televisions, websites, and telephone screens. And so, with the words *Alshaab yurid isqat alnizam*, "The people want to bring down the regime," scrawled across a schoolyard in Deraa, the Arab Spring flared to life in Syria.

Chapter Thirteen

October 10, 2013 12:41 p.m.

Nadia took a deep, ragged breath and straightened her sore back, staring into the flames as she stroked her father's green cap in her lap.

"Are you okay, my dear?" asked Ammo Mazen. While she'd been lost in painful memories, he'd been busy—a steaming kettle sat on the brazier, whistling softly.

Nadia blinked away tears. "I don't know what to do," she choked out.

"Now, now, things aren't as bad as we think they are," he said, pouring liquid from the kettle into two chipped, tulip-patterned mugs. "Drink this. I find that it calms the nerves."

Gratefully, Nadia took it and inhaled the delicate, flowery scent, the mug warming her cold fingers through the mittens. She recognized it at once. It was *zhourat* tea, made with marshmallow flowers, lemon balm, rose petals, chamomile, and other herbs. Nana made it often, and the thought nearly brought more tears. But she pushed them back and drank the soothing brew. Feeling a bit better, she watched Ammo Mazen remove a plastic bag from the leather rucksack that had been hidden beneath the cart. He took out stiff pieces of bread and held them over the fire with a metal skewer. Once they were toasted, he produced a tin of cheese and opened it with a rusty can opener. Nadia's stomach grumbled.

"Here you go," said Ammo Mazen, handing her a tin plate with a warm piece of bread slathered with soft white cheese.

"Thank you," she said, trying to mind her manners, at least a little, as she fell on the food like a lion tearing into a gazelle. She hadn't eaten cheese in months. It had become a luxury, like fruit, only affordable for the rich. Staples like vegetables and meat were hard to find, and bread. *Bread* . . . She unconsciously rubbed her thigh. The price of bread had skyrocketed, and it was because of this that she had this souvenir in her thigh, and the scars on her face. But with her stomach full, she felt a little better, her mind clearer. She leaned back and tried to make sense of what to do next. Staring down at her mittened hands, she recalled the message her family had left for her. *Your father will wait for you at Oncupinar border crossing, which faces Bab al-Salama on the Syrian side.* She had taken that route many times when her family had gone into the countryside for summer picnics, or on the rare occasion she'd accompanied her father and brothers to inspect a phosphate mine.

She sat up straight. "I have to find my father!" she murmured to herself.

"I know," said Ammo Mazen, between delicate, slow chews. "He is waiting for you at the border."

Nadia nodded. "You take the main road north out of the city and go past the ruins of Kharab Shams, right? Do you know how to go from there?" she asked hopefully.

"Yes," he said, then paused, a frown marring his brow. He blinked, appearing a bit befuddled as if he were putting together a particularly difficult puzzle. A fleeting look of calculation crossed his features, then he smiled. "I do."

"Will you tell me how?" she asked with growing excitement.

"I can do better than that," he said with a smile.

"How?" she asked.

"I will take you there," he replied.

"You will?" she whispered, her heart pounding. "But why?" she added, suddenly suspicious.

Ammo Mazen looked at her with a twinkle in his eyes. "I agreed to help you, so now I am committed to my promise. Plus, my errand is taking me north, and the border is not so far that I cannot take a detour."

It sounds logical, thought Nadia, weighing his words. And since she had no idea how to get there alone, she couldn't afford to pass up on his offer of help. "Thank you, Ammo," she said simply.

"But if we are to travel together," said Ammo Mazen, "you must pretend to be my granddaughter, and follow my instructions."

Nadia nodded, eyeing the cars with renewed hope, wondering if they could get one to work. The border was barely thirty miles away, a scenic drive that once took less than an hour to complete. Now, of course, it could take much, much longer. "What are we waiting for?" she cried, jumping up. "Let's go."

"Hold on, my dear," said Ammo Mazen. "It is not as simple as that. We must plan carefully."

"I know, I know," said Nadia, pacing. "But I'm sure we can find a car, or a truck."

Ammo Mazen sighed. "No automobiles. It is far too dangerous."

"But a car will be fastest," argued Nadia, folding her arms.

"There are hundreds of checkpoints throughout the city, and getting through them, especially in a car, is dangerous," said Ammo Mazen. "They can question you for hours, and if they don't like your answers they can hold you up even longer. Plus, I cannot leave Jamila and my things."

Nadia mutinously stared at the smelly donkey, snoring away with Mishmish curled up under her neck. *All he has is a bunch of junk,* she fumed. *Why is that so important?* She opened her mouth to tell him just that, then clamped it shut as she eyed the old man in his frayed clothes, weariness etched on his face.

Nadia, don't be so selfish, rebuked a voice inside her head, one that sounded like her mother. Her shoulders slumped in shame at the truth of the words. Ammo Mazen had offered to help her, and it was unfair to ask him to leave his faithful donkey. "So when do we leave?" she asked with more humility.

"I have found that the safest way to travel is in the protective embrace of darkness," he explained. "We rest by day and journey at night."

"But what if we're too late and I miss him at the border?" said Nadia.

"Don't worry, we will find him," said Ammo Mazen. "We know exactly where he will be, and he'll make it known he is looking for his daughter. Keep a positive heart and keep your faith in him who is greater than us all." Nadia nodded grudgingly. "By the way," he added, "do you have your identification card?"

Every Syrian citizen has a national identification card that displays the bearer's name, address, date of birth, national identification number, and photograph, as well as a bar code. In addition, it contains two peculiar administrative details: *imana*, which part of Syria one is from, and *qayd*, one's father's or grandfather's village or neighborhood of origin. With these two items, the cardholder's regional ties, ethnicity, and, by inference, religious group could be gleaned. Nadia shook her head. "No, my mother has it," she said.

"No matter," said Ammo Mazen, and as he was about to say more, a deep shuddering cough racked his slender frame. He pulled a snowy-white handkerchief from his coat pocket to cover his mouth. "Nadia," he wheezed. "Go . . . the cart . . . find my small leather bag . . . hurry."

Frightened, Nadia ran and dragged the tarp off the cart. She rifled through his belongings, tossing aside tools and dumping clothing, bags, and books onto the floor, until she spotted the small leather bag. She sprinted back while opening the zipper. "What do you need?" she asked, placing the collection of bottles, tubes, and small boxes onto the blanket.

With shaking fingers, he grabbed a dark brown bottle and unscrewed the cap. He shook out a pale blue pill, one of two that remained in the bottle, and swallowed it with a sip of tea. Eyes closed, he leaned back on the cushion, Nadia crouched beside him, heart racing. After a few strained minutes, his breathing finally eased.

"Are you all right?" whispered Nadia.

His eyes flickered open. "Yes, child. Old age, exhaustion, and this terrible war have taken their toll. I believe sleep will do me wonders. I suggest that you also rest up."

As the fire in the brazier burned down, Nadia lay cocooned in the blankets, watching the old man. After tucking the leather case beside him, he'd started snoring within minutes. *He's exhausted,* she thought, studying his sharp features. He was certainly old, older than Jiddo had been, and very thin, practically gaunt. She eyed the medicine bag and wondered what the pills were for; Jiddo had taken medicines for a variety of ailments.

Restless, she finally pushed aside the covers and wandered toward the cars, wishing she could just drive like the wind all the way to the border. A twinge at her knee made her pause at the door she'd seen earlier. Curiosity got the better of her, and she turned the knob, revealing a messy, cramped office. A metal desk stood against the far wall, stacked with receipts, manuals, and car parts. A phone sat on the corner and she reached for it instinctively. *Dead. Useless without electricity.* Disappointed, she was about to turn, when flames from the fire illuminated the wall, revealing a line of familiar faces. A thrill flared through her as she gazed at the faded posters.

Umm Kulthum stared down at her with arched brows. Many swore she was the best singer of the Arab world, her powerful voice bringing people to tears. Beside her stood willowy Fairuz, whose delicate melodies resonated with hope and love. Nadia's eyes roamed over the familiar faces, stopping at bright eyes rimmed with kohl: Carmen, the contestant from *Arab Idol* she had so admired. With a last glance, she gently pulled the door shut and limped to the fire.

She caught sight of the cart and stopped short, staring at the mess she'd made. Chagrined, she folded the rumpled clothes, lined up the tools, stacked plates and pots, and grouped cooking utensils back in their place. The brown-paper-wrapped package Alaa had given Ammo Mazen still sat snug at the back of the cart, tucked between dozens of books. As she lined up the tools, her sleeve caught along the side of the cart. To her surprise, as she pulled away a little door sprang open. From inside the hidden compartment tumbled a black velvet bag. With tentative fingers, she picked it up, and was surprised by its weight. Unable to resist, she pulled open the strings. She gasped. Inside were stacks of bills—American dollars, Euros, British pounds—and over a dozen gold bars: a small fortune. *What else is in there?* she thought, tempted to reach inside the compartment. Instead, she guiltily shoved the bag back inside and sealed the door, which lined up with the grain of the wood, impossible to detect without close inspection. Heart pounding, she glanced back at Ammo Mazen. He was still asleep. But suspicion flared in her mind. *Who has this kind of money? Where did he get it?*

All she knew about him was that he'd grown up in a small village in the mountains and had been a fisherman and a book repairer. But so far, he hadn't done anything but help her. For now, she had no choice but to trust him. There was no way to navigate through the city on her own to reach her family. *Family. Where are they? Did they get caught in the fighting?* She stood, fingering the silver pin on her coat lapel, wishing there was something, *anything*, that would take her mind away from her tortured thoughts. She wished the old man had a radio or CD player so that she could listen to some music. Instead, in the cart there were books, over fifty of them, mostly old and tattered. Over the years her mother had bought her dozens of books on all sorts of topics, hoping she'd be a reader like her brothers, but she'd only really been interested in fashion and gossip magazines.

She ran a finger along the dusty old spines and one caught her eye, a tall, slim book with gilded edges. Gently tugging it out, she saw that the cover was practically falling apart. The title read *Alef Layla.* That rang a bell. It was a collection of fantastical stories collected from the Middle East and India. It had the same title as a blockbuster movie from a few years earlier, *One Thousand and One Nights*. She carried the book back to the fire and flipped it open to the first delicate page, written in an elegant script of old Arabic. Lyrical words flowed across her tongue and she fell into the familiar story of the cunning Scheherazade, the brave queen who told her husband, the king, a different tale every night to keep him from killing her.

She'd finished "The Merchant and the Demon" and was deep into "Ali Baba and the Forty Thieves" when she heard Jamila snort. Awake and on her feet, the donkey snorted again, and before Nadia could make out what the silly animal was doing, Jamila trotted forward and nudged Ammo Mazen in the side with her head, waking him. Mishmish had made his way over to Nadia and stood, head cocked at an angle.

"What's wrong, my dear?" he said, grabbing his spectacles as he sat up. He closed his eyes and listened. Nadia froze, and from deep within the ground, she felt it. A low rumble. "We need to leave," said Ammo Mazen, exhaustion still lining his face. "Quickly now, collect your things. We must find a safer place to find shelter till night falls."

Nadia grabbed Mishmish and gently put him in his bag, wondering if there was a safe place anywhere in the city. She folded up the blankets and stacked them in the cart along with the book she'd taken.

"Did you enjoy the story?" asked Ammo Mazen, putting Jamila's harness in place.

Nadia nodded a bit guiltily, thinking that perhaps she shouldn't have taken his book without asking permission.

"Scheherazade was a woman to be commended

and admired," said Ammo Mazen, hooking up the cart. "She took on the king and outwitted him with her intelligence."

Nadia smiled in relief, realizing he didn't mind. She put the visor over her cap.

"We need some speed, my sweet," Ammo Mazen whispered into Jamila's ear. Muscles tense, the donkey pranced through the door as soon as Ammo Mazen rolled up the metal shutter. "We will move further north and find another spot to hide away for nightfall."

Nadia glanced up to see that the sun was still high in the sky, indicating that it was past noon. From the west came a familiar *pop*, then another, followed by a fiery explosion. Rapidly, she calculated. "The rebels are firing *jarra* about half a mile away," she called up to Ammo Mazen.

He pursed his lips and muttered, "Those homemade hell cannons are unpredictable and dangerous."

Nadia nodded, lips puckered with worry. Blue propane cylinders filled with nails and ball bearings, *jarra* were notorious for going off course, killing and maiming whoever had the misfortune of standing nearby—rebels themselves or innocent civilians. She couldn't help but think of the battalion of women they'd met that morning. *I hope they're all right. . . .* Allah, *please keep them safe.* Cold wind whipped by, numbing her face. She pulled down her hat, hiding her ears and neck. Jamila slowed to go around a broken-down Jeep from which a group of well-dressed women and children descended.

"Can you help us?" called out the woman who'd been driving.

"My apologies, but I know nothing of fixing automobiles," said Ammo Mazen.

"What's happening, brother?" asked a woman Nana's age.

"A battle is stirring in the west," he explained. "Army and rebels are at each other's throats."

"It's not like Ghouta, is it?" asked the old woman, her face creased with fear. "How can Bashar be so unmerciful and cruel?"

Nadia froze. Two months ago, a sarin gas attack had killed over a thousand civilians in a rebel stronghold outside Damascus, called Ghouta.

"No, sister, thank *Allah* there are no reports of chemical weapons being used," said Ammo Mazen.

The old woman's face tightened in disgust. "That American president, what did he say? If the devil Assad uses chemical weapons, that would cross a red line and would have consequences! Ha, the line has been crossed, but he and the west do nothing but watch us die."

Ammo Mazen nodded, cutting off her diatribe. "You must hurry now. Take the little ones and find a hiding place. The best is to find a room in the lower level or basement."

"Thank you, brother—may *Allah* be with you!" she shouted as they moved on.

"Where are we going?" asked Nadia, trying to figure out where they were. A deserted school appeared on their right, but it wouldn't offer much protection since the entire face of the building had been sheared off.

"I know of a place," said Ammo Mazen, pulling out his compass.

Jamila turned off the main boulevard and merged onto a side street. Zigzagging through a maze of narrow alleys, she slowed as one ended in a quaint cul-de-sac. A small mosque sat in a courtyard, enclosed by a metal fence. Sturdy, abandoned apartment buildings, scarred by explosions, shouldered it on either side.

"We'll stop here," said Ammo Mazen, guiding Jamila into the courtyard. He pulled up next to a fountain filled with rainwater. With a snuffle, Jamila eagerly dipped her muzzle inside and drank.

Nadia gingerly stepped down, holding Mishmish close to her chest while scanning every corner of the courtyard, looking for any sign of movement. The air seemed heavier and the sounds of battles muted.

"I know the *imam* in charge," said Ammo Mazen, walking briskly toward the mosque, where a flock of pigeons roosted atop the dome. "He runs the orphanage there." He angled his head toward a squat building rising beyond a small stretch of scrubby grass. The old man paused at the door and stood a moment, listening. Nadia followed, the eerie silence sending a rush of goose bumps along her arm.

Ammo Mazen gently pushed open the door, revealing a darkened hall, the floor covered in faded green carpet. "They've left," he said, shoulders drooping, face pale.

He needs to rest, thought Nadia.

"I know he was thinking about it, but I guess they

couldn't stay any longer." He headed back to the fountain. "Come," he instructed, pulling Jamila's head from the water.

Irritated, she snorted, spraying water all over Nadia. "Oooh," she grumbled, eyeing the cantankerous beast, who seemed to be laughing at her. It was because of the smelly beast that they were going on foot, and now *this*.

"The most secure place will be the orphanage," said Ammo Mazen. "There is a big hall where the cart will fit."

As they approached the wide double doors, pockmarked with bullet holes, a voice from the window above boomed out. "Stop! Don't enter if you value your life."

Nadia stopped dead in her tracks. Her head jerked up toward the window where the barrel of a rifle was aimed down at them.

Chapter Fourteen

October 10, 2013 3:52 p.m.

"Go away," came a bellicose voice from above.

"We don't want you around here!" shouted another.

Nadia froze, but Ammo Mazen nudged her to get behind the cart.

"We mean you no harm," said Ammo Mazen, his tone cordial. "We were just looking for Imam Ali. Do you know where he is?"

Silence resonated above, followed by intense whispering. Nadia caught snatches of hushed words.

"He says he knows your imam. . . ."

"He's lying. . . . Don't trust him. . . ."

Ammo Mazen stared at the window, a shrewd look on his face. "Imam Ali and I are good friends and I've brought food to share."

Nadia frowned. *Why is he offering our food? We should just leave these crazy people alone!*

A scuffle sounded from above, then a loud "Go away!"

An annoyed whisper interrupted, "But they have *food.*"

"Be quiet," hissed the first.

Then the muzzle of the gun shifted and wobbled. "Give me that!" the second voice yelped.

"Ow," came a howl of indignation. The weapon jerked sideways and tilted down.

"Move away," grunted Ammo Mazen just as a large rifle with a wooden butt came tumbling through the air. Nadia ducked for cover beneath the cart as the gun landed with a sharp clang against the stones. This was not the time to die from an accidental discharge.

Ammo Mazen grabbed the weapon and stared at it in amazement. "An StG 44," he muttered. "German made, from World War Two. Very rare indeed."

Nadia stared at how easily he checked the magazine clip, which was empty. *How does he know so much about guns?*

"Look at what you made me do!" hollered a furious voice.

"Stop squabbling and open the door," Ammo Mazen ordered. "We are not here to hurt you, but to help."

After another round of muffled quarreling, footsteps approached. A series of bolts thudded and the double doors creaked open. From behind the cart Nadia spotted a boy, no older than eight or nine. Hands on his hips, he stood imperious, his round frame encased in a loose, not particularly clean soldier's coat, which he'd tightened with a belt. He scowled, the expression almost comical on his round, dimpled face, framed by too-long, silky brown hair.

From behind him, a lanky boy stepped forward. This one was in his early teens. "Who are you and what do you want?" he asked, his thin features pinched, long dark hair tied back. He wore a simple white tunic and pants, a faded, red-and-white-checked *keffiyeh* scarf draped over his shoulders.

"Yeah, what do you want?" asked the soldier boy, pushing out his chest.

"Now, is this a way to talk to your elders?" asked Ammo Mazen, eyebrows raised.

Color blazed across the older boy's cheeks and he lowered his gaze.

"This is war," blurted the little boy. "Not a time for being nice. We have to protect ourselves."

Surprised by his audacity, Nadia stared at him, eyes narrowed.

Ammo Mazen smiled wearily. "You have a point there, young man."

"Apologies," muttered the older boy, bowing his head. "But he is right. We had to be careful."

"Where is Imam Ali?" asked Ammo Mazen.

"He left, a month ago," said the older boy, eyes shifting.

"And the students?" asked Ammo Mazen.

"They left with him," said the boy.

"Where did they go?" asked Ammo Mazen.

"To the border," said the boy, "to Turkey."

"And you stayed?" prodded Ammo Mazen.

The boy nodded. Ammo Mazen was about to ask something else when the little boy interrupted. "Can I have my gun back?"

The old man hesitated. "Where are the bullets?"

The boy scuffed his foot against the floor. "I, uh . . .

don't really have any. It was my grandfather's. He gave it to me before he left to join the rebels." Ammo Mazen nodded and handed it back. "So do you really have food?" asked the little boy, hugging the rifle to his chest.

"I do, but how about you let us come inside and we chat a bit, then we'll eat?"

The taller one hesitated. "Did you really know Imam Ali?" he asked.

"Yes, since he was a little boy," answered Ammo Mazen. "His mother, Zainab, was a teacher. She and her husband, Majid, were very proud of Ali's work."

The boy nodded, shoulders easing. Doors pushed aside, he showed them into a long hall, filled with small desks. Ammo Mazen led Jamila inside and Nadia followed, Mishmish sticking his head out of the bag.

The older boy jumped back in surprise. "You have a cat."

"Uh, yeah," muttered Nadia at the obvious.

"Can I hold it?" he asked, surprising her.

Nadia gave him a measured look. Finally, she handed Mishmish to him.

A smile broke out over his melancholy features as

he sank his face into the tolerant cat's fur. "What's his name?"

"Mishmish," replied Nadia.

"Good name," he said solemnly. "Cats were loved by the Prophet, peace be upon him, you know." Nadia shrugged.

He continued, "Once he cut off the sleeve of his prayer robe rather than wake Muezza, his favorite cat."

This kid and Razan would get along, thought Nadia, taking Mishmish and putting him on the floor so he could go explore.

"So you've been here these last months?" Ammo Mazen asked the older boy, who ducked his head and nodded. "Why didn't you leave with the others?"

"I needed to stay here," he mumbled.

"But it's dangerous for just the two of you to be here, alone."

"Oh, I'm not with him," said the little boy, reaching down to scratch Mishmish under the chin.

Ammo Mazen folded his arms, face settling into a serious expression. "Sit," he ordered, pointing to a set of chairs. "And tell me your names."

• • •

After fifteen minutes of interrogation, they learned that the older one, Tarek, had been at the school since he was five. One of over a dozen orphans, he was being trained by Imam Ali to become a religious scholar. The little soldier, Basel, was eight, and on his way to a rebel battalion on the eastern front to join his grandfather. Casually, as if he'd been talking about the weather, he'd explained that the building he'd been living in with his grandmother had been hit by a *barmeela* a few weeks before. She had not made it out. He'd run away from the neighbors who'd taken him in, to find his grandfather. His parents, he'd added in a matter-of-fact tone, had been killed in a car accident when he was a baby. He'd stopped at the mosque to rest for the night, and stumbled onto Tarek.

Nadia stared at him, horrified by his story. Her heart softened as she realized he must still be in shock.

"Sir, where's this food you were talking about?" asked Basel pointedly.

"I don't have much, but what I have we will all share," said Ammo Mazen, wincing slightly as he rose from his chair.

Nadia noticed that his shoulders were stooped and

his steps were slow. "Let me help you," she said as the boys followed him to the cart.

"Thank you, dear girl," he said, pushing aside the tarp, revealing that in their mad dash, the things Nadia had neatly organized were a jumbled mess. Ammo Mazen reached for a lumpy bag and extracted a small pouch. As he bent down to retrieve the leather rucksack from beneath the cart, the brown-paper-wrapped package tumbled to the floor. Tarek quickly bent to pick it up and handed it back.

Ammo Mazen gave him an appreciative smile, securing it safely under the tarp. "Thank you. I have to deliver that before we head north, and it mustn't get damaged."

The kitchen was empty, cupboards bare, but there was still gas left in the cylinders for the stove. When Basel saw the meager fare Ammo Mazen laid out on the counter—half a packet of dried beans, some wrinkled carrots, an onion, and stale bread—he sighed.

"I can help," he said, pulling a slingshot from his stained pack. Soon after disappearing, he returned, three scrawny pigeons tucked under his arm.

"You are a useful young lad," laughed Ammo

Mazen, taking the birds to dress them. The heart and liver he tossed to Mishmish, who ate happily under the table, purring contentedly.

Nadia took off her mittens and helped cut up the vegetables.

"Nice color," said Basel, pausing from humming a patriotic marching song to admire the glitter in her nail polish.

"Thanks," said Nadia, careful with the knife so it wouldn't chip her nails.

The little boy sat next to her, drawing pictures in the dust using a stick of wood. Tarek, meanwhile, lugged in a bucket, sloshing with water from the well. Half he poured into a pot on the stove. When steam rose from the tin pot's depths, Ammo Mazen added a bouillon cube and the pigeon pieces, vegetables, and dried beans. Then he opened the small leather pouch and pulled out a bottle. As he unscrewed the lid, Nadia felt the breath leave her chest. She grabbed the edge of the table, overwhelmed by the memory of being in Nana's kitchen, helping her prepare magnificent feasts. She inhaled the familiar mixture of allspice, cardamom, black pepper, cinnamon, coriander, and cumin rising from the bottle.

"My personal combination of *baharat,*" Ammo Mazen said, adding a heaping teaspoon to the pot.

"That sure does smell good," said Basel, rocking back and forth on his heels as he and Tarek stared intently. "My nana was the best cook in the world," he added wistfully, a faraway look in his eyes.

"Mine too," said Nadia, giving him a smile.

While the stew bubbled merrily and mouth-watering smells invaded the kitchen, the kids set the table. From the corner of her eye, Nadia spotted Ammo Mazen pouring himself a cup of water and swallowing a pill. He stood at the window, gazing out over the courtyard, a thoughtful frown on his face.

Within an hour they were sitting around the table, preparing to dip a piece of Ammo Mazen's dry bread into the delicious broth.

"Wait," cried Tarek. As the others paused, he recited: "*Bismillah wa ala barakatillah.* In the name of *Allah* and with the blessings of *Allah.*"

As they dove into the food, Ammo Mazen sat, deep in thought.

He looks drained, thought Nadia. Although he'd

said he was hungry, half of his stew remained.

"Are you going to eat that, sir?" asked Basel, eyes hopeful.

"No, you may have it," said Ammo Mazen with a smile, pushing it toward him.

The boy didn't need to be told twice, and he sank his teeth into a tiny pigeon leg. "This is so much better cooked."

"You ate it raw?" asked Nadia in horror.

He shrugged. "You have to survive."

"You shouldn't stuff yourself," admonished Tarek, staring in disapproval at the boy. "It is advised that eating less is healthier; a third of your stomach should contain food, a third water, and a third air."

"Well, my stomach has been full of air for days, so I'm filling it up now," said Basel. "I'm sure the Prophet wouldn't mind, sir."

While they bickered, Ammo Mazen put on his glasses and reached inside his vest. From inside emerged a small black book. Gently, he flipped through the pages, pausing to jot down notes. With a deep sigh, he looked up at them. "Before leaving the city I have to take care of a few things," he said.

Nadia frowned, scrunching up her father's woolen cap in her hands. "How long will that take?"

"Don't worry," said Ammo Mazen. "The people I need to see are on our path out of the city."

Nadia wanted to argue, but held her tongue. After all, she was the one interrupting his schedule. She had to be patient, a virtue she was unfamiliar with.

"But for now," continued Ammo Mazen, "there's still another hour or so before sunset. My sleep has been sparse, so I must rest."

"There are rooms at the back," said Tarek. "I can show you."

"Thank you, son," said Ammo Mazen, following him.

Basel muffled a burp and collected the bowls to be washed. "That was the best thing I've eaten in a while," he said happily.

Since the kitchen was still the warmest place in the building, Nadia decided to bring back her bedroll and the book. While she made herself comfortable, Basel slumped down beside her.

"What's that?" he asked, pointing to the leather-bound folio.

"A book," said Nadia, irritated.

"What kind of book?"

She rolled her eyes. *"Alef Layla."*

"Never heard of it," he said.

"How can you not have heard of it?" she asked.

He shrugged. "We couldn't really afford storybooks, and my grandmother didn't have that much time to read to me."

"Oh," she said, surprised to feel sympathy. "Well, how about I read to you?"

"Would you, ma'am?" asked Basel, his long-lashed brown eyes eager. "That would be really great."

"Okay, but first, stop calling me ma'am," said Nadia. She flipped open to a tale she knew he would enjoy, of the great adventurer Sinbad the Sailor, who goes on an epic quest to find riches while defeating monsters and villains along the way.

Chapter Fifteen

October 10, 2013 7:03 p.m.

H*e really needed the rest,* thought Nadia, taking a measured look at the dark shadows under Ammo Mazen's eyes.

"Which way are you headed exactly, sir?" Basel asked as he watched Ammo Mazen and Nadia pack up the cart.

"Northeast," said Ammo Mazen, tucking the tarp along the edges of the cart.

"Can I go with you to the Old City?" asked Basel. "The rebel group my grandfather joined, the Freedom Army, is there."

Nadia looked at him in surprise. *Such a little boy joining a rebel group? That's not safe.*

"Unfortunately, we won't be going that far east," said Ammo Mazen, giving him a sympathetic look.

An odd feeling of guilt tickled Nadia's mind. It

didn't feel right to leave the boys behind. *They're not my problem,* she reminded herself. She had to focus on getting to the border without distractions.

"Can I come with you as far as you go?" he pleaded.

The old man paused from tying down the tarp. He glanced from Nadia and back to the little boy, a fleeting look of calculation crossing his features. "Certainly," he finally said. "But if you are to travel with me, you must pretend to be my grandson and listen to my instructions. Agreed?"

The same rules he set for me, thought Nadia as Basel nodded happily.

"And what about you?" He turned to Tarek. "The battle may push this way soon. Are you sure you want to remain here, alone?"

Tarek nodded, eyes downcast.

"Why?" Nadia couldn't help but ask. "You're an orphan, right? What's here for you?"

Tarek's cheeks flushed. "I have to stay."

"Have to?" probed Ammo Mazen.

"He thinks his mother's coming back to get him, sir," said Basel.

"You be quiet!" cried Tarek, fists clenched.

"You call out for her in your sleep," said Basel.

"Your mother?" asked Ammo Mazen, his voice soft.

Tarek stared down at his feet, face stony.

"When did you see her last?" Ammo Mazen gently prodded.

"When she left me here," muttered Tarek.

"When you were five?" said Nadia. "That was like ten years ago."

"Nine years ago," said Tarek, glaring at her.

"And you haven't heard from her in all these years?" asked Ammo Mazen. When Tarek shook his head, he continued, "I understand your desire to stay, son, but the city is getting more dangerous by the day, and without food you will not survive. When your mother hears that Imam Ali has left for Turkey, she'll look for you there."

"I have to wait," said Tarek. "I'm old enough now, and it's my duty to take care of her."

Nadia stared at him as if he had rocks for brains. *His mother dumped him here, and now he wants to take care of her?*

Tarek must have seen the look of disgust on her face. "It doesn't matter what she *did*, or why she did it. We *must* respect our parents, mothers above all. It's written in the Quran that heaven lies beneath our mothers' feet."

When Basel muttered, "He's a regular preacher," Ammo Mazen gave him an admonishing look.

Nadia stared at Tarek, an alien sensation bubbling up inside of her. *Shame.* She lowered her gaze, realizing she'd never bothered to think about all the things her parents had done for her all these years.

"You must do as your heart guides you," said Ammo Mazen, clasping the boy's shoulder. "But I leave having advised you that this may not be the best decision."

"I appreciate that, uncle," said Tarek, his voice soft.

Nadia pulled on her visor and, unable to resist, glanced back at the orphanage. A pale face hung in the second-story window, watching them go. *He should have come with us,* she thought.

"That Sinbad the Sailor is amazing," Basel said, interrupting her thoughts. "What an adventure, to land on an island with giant birds, a valley of snakes, and treasures!"

Nadia couldn't help but smile at his enthusiasm.

He'd begged her to keep reading, and she'd done so, both lost in the book as Scheherazade spun her magic over them. Then finally, they'd slept. Her smile evaporated as she remembered that Tarek had sat nearby, Mishmish in his lap, smiling at the sailor's misfortunes.

"That's one of my favorites too," said Ammo Mazen with a chuckle as he tucked his compass back into his vest pocket. "Though I've always wished to find Aladdin's magic lamp with a *jinni* to give me three wishes."

They continued their conversation in hushed whispers, tensing as the scream of a jet passed above. But no sounds of bombing echoed in its wake, so they continued through a desolate neighborhood, illuminated by the silvery light of the full moon. On both sides of the road rose skeletal buildings. It was a scene that would have fit on the moon itself: gray and lifeless. Nadia swallowed, her throat suddenly parched, a sense of foreboding stealing over her. She stared at Ammo Mazen, wanting to ask him how they were going to exit the city. But he had slowed, eyes focused along the narrow road they traveled. About a hundred feet away, it met a wider street. He stopped, put a finger to his lips, and waved at them to slow down. Ten feet from the intersection, he motioned for them to stand still. He extracted a long wooden stick from the cart, a rearview mirror attached at its end. He crept forward and angled the mirror toward the intersection.

Nadia caught a glimpse of bright lights and a group of soldiers reflected on its silver surface. *A checkpoint.*

"We can't go this way," whispered Ammo Mazen. "I don't recognize any of them."

Nadia frowned, wondering how he could know the hundreds of rebel groups that had carved out sections of the city to rule. It was yet another mystery about him.

Through a series of streets, they hurried toward what looked like a long stretch of darkness. Nadia wondered where they were, and tried to imagine a map of the city. Her eyes focused and she realized they were on the edge of the Saad al-Ansari district, on the western side of the sinewy Queiq River. It was also called the River of Martyrs, Nadia had learned, after a hundred men and boys were found in its depths, hands tied behind their backs, executed by government forces. A thousand years ago, the river had burst its banks and swept away European crusader camps, helping save a besieged Aleppo. Now the river was a trickle compared with what it had been, its power diverted by a dam built at its source in Turkey.

And there was only one way to cross from one side of the city to the other from this point. "Bustan al-Qasr crossing?" choked out Nadia, horrified.

"Yes, I'm afraid we will have to pass through there," said Ammo Mazen, handing around a water bottle.

"My father told me it's manned on the western side by Syrian army forces and by rebels on the eastern side," said Nadia. "People crossing there are targeted by snipers, so it's been nicknamed the Death Crossing."

"Snipers?" gasped Basel, choking on a gulp of water.

"Don't worry," said Ammo Mazen, though his face was serious in the silver light of the moon. "I've done this many times. The thugs who once ran the checkpoint have been replaced by a more agreeable lot. For now, let's rest a bit." He turned toward the cart and lifted the tarp.

As Basel pulled Nadia toward a spot beneath a tree, she glimpsed Ammo Mazen reaching into his small leather bag for his bottle of pills.

With the recent rains, the park bordering the river was lush and green. Let loose, Jamila happily ate her fill of soft, fresh grass, while Mishmish, curtailed by a length of rope tied around his neck, lazed beside Nadia and Basel, who sat with their backs against a tree trunk. Nadia stretched, feeling a twinge in her thigh, which she rubbed away with a grimace.

"So," said Basel, fashioning a sort of basket out of leaves, "what happened to your leg?"

She opened her mouth to tell him to mind his own business. Instead, somehow, the dark, tangled memories came tumbling out. "When food was hard to find in Salaheddine, my mother heard that a shipment of flour had made it in. Bread would be available, though it would be expensive. They sent my cousin Malik with money. But since I'd been cooped up in the house for months, I wanted to go too. They wouldn't let me, so I snuck out and joined him while he was standing in a line that stretched over ten blocks."

She trailed off as an image of the day came back . . . a perfect mix of warm sun and cool breezes. Instead of grumbling about the wait, the people had been laughing and joking as the yeasty smell of baking bread wafted down the street.

"Then what happened?" prodded Basel, swatting Jamila's head away as she tried to eat his leaf basket.

"That's when we heard the helicopters," said Nadia. "I don't remember much of what happened after that, only that Malik and his friend carried me home."

"A bomb fell on you?" Basel whistled.

"No, a bomb did *not* fall on me." She grimaced. "The bomb landed on a car across the street from me. The shrapnel hit me." She didn't tell him about the excruciating surgery Khala Lina had performed on the dining room table because they couldn't go to the hospital. Or of the months she'd taken painkillers when they could find them, and struggled to heal and walk properly again. And how she'd started sleeping under her bed, and refused to leave the house. "We found out later that Assad's regime was bombing bakeries . . . to starve and kill his own people."

"It's over there," said Ammo Mazen, pointing toward the end of the street. It was strewn with discarded clothes, garbage, and an old television set. "Take a deep breath and relax," he instructed. "If they ask, tell them I'm your grandfather and we're going to stay with relatives since our house was bombed. Okay?" Both nodded and fell in beside the cart as Jamila trotted forward.

This is it, thought Nadia, wishing they didn't have to go this way. But it was one of the few access points from the western side of the city, under government control, to the eastern side, controlled by rebels. However, the boundaries changed as battles were fought and won. Goose bumps rose along her arms as they emerged onto the western end of Karaj al-Hajaz street in the once vibrant Bustan al-Qasr neighborhood. This leg of the road was the infamous Death Crossing that desperate souls braved every day to reach friends and family on the other side; to attend the university, back when it was still open; to go to work, if still employed; or to find food. A street vendor hawked Korean-made generators on the corner, a hot commodity these days. Much of the business being conducted was through barter, since people's cash had disappeared. An old man hurried by, gently guiding his wife along.

They passed a bus, its tires gone, blocking half the road. Beyond it rose the national flag, fixed to the Syrian army checkpoint, surrounded by sandbags. A short line formed at the front, where a group of men in black shirts and camouflage pants screamed insults at a young man who stood trembling in front of them, holding out his papers. Basel gulped, and began to hum a jaunty tune. Nadia grabbed his hand and squeezed, thinking how the feisty boy reminded her of Yusuf. Trailing off on the last note, he straightened, arms naked without his rifle, which Ammo Mazen had hidden beneath the cart.

A bald, muscular man in white tennis shoes stepped forward, ice-blue eyes trained on Ammo Mazen. Behind him hung a portrait of the president. Under it someone had scrawled: *If not for the fear of God, I would worship you, Bashar, although you are a human being.* Revulsion filled Nadia and she wished she could tear it to shreds.

"Identification cards," the soldier barked.

Eyes downcast, Ammo Mazen presented his to him, while Nadia peered at the handful of other men from beneath her visor. They were smoking and trading jokes. One of them had an image of Bashar al-Assad tattooed on his bicep. Realization dawned that they weren't in military uniform. Fear curled up her back, like the icy fingers of a ghost. *Shabiha . . .*

"Your family name is Kader?" asked the man. Ammo Mazen nodded. "Your *qayd*?" the man asked.

"Born and raised in Aleppo for ten generations," answered Ammo Mazen.

Aleppo? thought Nadia. She remembered him saying he'd been born in a small village in the mountains. There were no mountains in Aleppo. But this was not the time to ponder such things.

"Who are they?" he asked, squinting at Nadia and Basel, who tried to look as meek as possible.

"My grandchildren," said Ammo Mazen, pushing them forward. Nadia tensed.

"Where are their identification cards?" the soldier asked, his stance relaxing a tiny bit.

Nadia realized what Ammo Mazen was doing. He was using them as a shield: to show that two children and a feeble old man couldn't possibly be a threat.

"I'm afraid they were destroyed when our home was attacked by those ruthless rebel scum," spat Ammo Mazen.

Even though Nadia knew he was acting, she couldn't help but feel angry at him for maligning the rebels.

"He's not on the list, so I guess we can't arrest him," said a laughing soldier with a bandage over his face, holding a pile of papers. He did a perfunctory inspection of the cart, flipping up the tarp and poking through the meager belongings and old books.

"I don't know," mused the blue-eyed man. "We may have to take in his ID for verification. It may take a few days, you know. . . ."

"Did you work for the rebels?" said the bandaged man, giving his cohort a wink.

Nadia tensed. *Dangerous,* a voice hissed inside her head. The wrong answer could get you taken to detention, or worse.

"No, I'm but a poor book repairer," said Ammo Mazen meekly, pulling a small paperback book from his satchel. "This may help clear things up."

The soldier took it as if it were a smelly piece of dung. From the middle, he took out two crisp bills. Nadia squinted. *American dollars!* He tossed the book away and slipped the money into his pocket. "You can go," he said, and stepped back.

Legs trembling, Nadia grabbed Basel's arm, and they hurried beside the cart. Barely a hundred yards away, behind another mountain of sandbags, stood six men in a mixture of civilian and military clothes, checking the papers for a beat-up old Jeep.

"*Salaam*, brothers," Ammo Mazen called out as the Jeep left. "What a lovely gift of rain *Allah* has been providing us."

"Something he should have sent years ago," grumbled a bearded young man.

"Don't take the Lord's name in vain," replied one of his companions, eyes stern.

"Is Dr. Saleem not on post tonight?" asked Ammo Mazen.

"You know Dr. Saleem?" asked the bearded man, the tension in his face easing a bit.

"I used to work at the university where he taught history," said Ammo Mazen.

The man's stance softened further. "He's not here tonight. Who are you?" he asked.

"My name is Mazen Kader. *Barmeela* destroyed our home, but thanks to *Allah*, we managed to escape with our lives and a few meager belongings. We are going to my sister's house near the Old City."

"Identification papers?"

Ammo Mazen handed him his identification card. "Unfortunately, we couldn't find my grandchildren's papers in the rubble. Mine was in my wallet."

"I hardly think he and the children are Assad's spies," scoffed the young man, eyes softening as he elbowed his bearded friend.

Nadia and Basel returned a shaky smile, playing their part, as the men quickly examined the cart.

"Keep out of sight of the radio tower!" they called out as Nadia and her companions moved on. "A bastard Syrian army sniper takes particular delight in shooting children."

"Come quickly, children," said Ammo Mazen as they scurried toward billowing sheets, strung up along the road to protect travelers from the tower on the other side.

Nadia needed no urging as she sidestepped pools of blood—some dried up and blackened, others still bright red and wet.

"Where are we going?" grumbled Nadia, wondering what stupid errand was so important to the old man. According to her watch it was nearly ten, and her leg ached horribly. They'd been wandering the back streets and every little sound set her nerves on edge.

"It's not far," said Ammo Mazen, pausing to squint down a shadowy street. "Basel, can you tell me what the sign over there says?"

Basel narrowed his gaze. "It's some kind of furniture store, sir," he said. "The sign has no name, just the picture of a cedar tree."

"Good," said Ammo Mazen, and directed them to hide behind a cluster of steel drums lined up beside a metalwork shop. After making sure that Nadia, Basel, Jamila, and the cart were hidden, he hurried to the store and knelt beneath the sign. When he returned, Nadia saw a candle sputtering on the step.

"What's that?" asked Nadia, confused.

"It's a signal for my contact," said Ammo Mazen, settling down beside them. He began to cough, and used his handkerchief to muffle the sound. He pulled his threadbare coat tighter and closed his eyes.

More waiting, thought Nadia, as Basel drew on the ground with a piece of charcoal he'd found. Frustrated, she stared at the lonely candle flame, dancing in the darkness.

Chapter Sixteen

April 27, 2012

"Bashar is altogether a different beast." Jiddo's voice was heavy with worry. Nadia glanced at her grandfather, surprised again at how frail he'd become. The tall, robust man she'd grown up with was now a shrunken, faded version of himself who existed on a ration of medicines. And these days he appeared on edge, confused, as he watched the world as he'd known it disintegrate before his eyes. "He'll not let Syria slip from his fingers like those other foolish rulers," he continued. "Even though the world is pressuring Bashar to step down, including that President Obama of America."

Nadia's father sighed. "I met a few of our business partners over dinner last night. Many of them still support Assad—their livelihoods are linked to the government."

Nadia set a pot of tea on the table, eavesdropping as the grown-ups sat around the living room. Jad sat in the corner, quietly surfing the Internet, face pensive. Over the past year Nadia's interest in the Arab Spring had grown by necessity, since everyone at school was talking about it. After government troops gunned down protestors in Deraa, part of the Syrian army had revolted, splitting off to form the Free Syrian Army. Hundreds of rebel groups had sprung up around the country, including among the Kurdish people in the north. They all had their own agendas and ideologies; the only thing in common was a hatred for the Assad regime and the desire to bring it down.

"He's terrified," said Ammo Hadi in disgust. "And in order to maintain power he'll do anything. You saw the videos coming out of the city of Homs. He killed innocent civilians for protesting, just like his father did in Hama back in the 1980s."

He's right, thought Nadia, being more helpful than usual by passing out cups of tea. Unlike other authoritarian rulers, like Ben Ali of Tunisia, who ran away to Saudi Arabia; or Egypt's Hosni Mubarak, who was put on trial; or Libya's Muammar Qaddafi, who was killed,

Bashar al-Assad had dug in his heels, keeping a death grip on power over Syria.

"And the United Nations' cease-fire was a total failure," said Nadia's mother. "Bashar, with Russian and Iranian support, still claims that he controls the country and that nothing is wrong."

"And the rebels are shouting as loud as they can that government forces are slaughtering civilians and attacking rebel strongholds," said Nadia's father. "It's a stalemate. And with foreign embassies closing in droves, there's no one to see the truth of what is happening here."

"What does the United Nations think?" said Khala Lina. "They sent in six peacekeepers to monitor twenty-three million people, over hundreds of thousands of square miles. Ridiculous!"

"And to think we are in this mess because Bashar became president by accident," grunted Ammo Hadi. "If his older brother, groomed for the presidency, hadn't died in the car crash, Bashar would still be just an eye doctor."

"No point in dwelling on that," said Nadia's father. "His brother would probably have been as bad. As soon as Hafez finished burying him, he was getting Bashar ready for the presidential throne."

Nadia frowned, wondering how a doctor, sworn to protect the sanctity of life, had turned on his own people like a bloodthirsty vampire.

Ammo Zayn took a sip of tea and finally got in a word. "A group of *mukhabarat* showed up at the factory this morning."

"What?" said Khala Shakira, shocked. "You didn't tell me that."

"I didn't want to worry you, my dear," said Ammo Zayn.

Nadia's father frowned at his younger brother. "You should have told me immediately. What did they want?"

"You were out, so was Hadi," said Ammo Zayn. "They wanted to know about an old friend of mine, from my university days. I told them I hadn't seen him in years, or talked to him."

"That's good," said Ammo Hadi. "We do not want our family under their scrutiny."

"It's okay, brother, you worry too much," said Ammo Zayn.

Jiddo closed his eyes and leaned back in his favorite chair. "Unlike people in other countries in the region, we Syrians have had a good life. Why experiment with something that could be worse? These rebels should go away."

"But the swell of rage from Deraa is spilling over," said Nana, who'd been sitting quietly beside Nadia's mother. "The people are no longer cowering, despite Bashar's fist."

"The demonstrations in Aleppo are getting bigger and bigger," Jad piped up.

Jiddo just wants to stick his head in the sand, like an ostrich, and make all the commotion go away, thought Nadia, worry nibbling at her insides. *Nana is right; the Syrian people are no longer staying silent.*

Chapter Seventeen

October 10, 2013 11:22 p.m.

W*e could have been halfway to Turkey by now, but no, we're wasting time on some stupid errand,* Nadia thought for the millionth time, huddled behind the drums, her patience spent. Mishmish kept growling, wanting out, but Nadia was afraid to release him. What if he disappeared again? She knew he didn't need to pee; he'd done that an hour or so ago. So she put her hand in the sack and tried to soothe him with a lengthy scratch under the chin, the way Tarek had done. *He should have come with us,* she thought with a pang of remorse. *How is he going to survive on his own?*

Basel was snuggled up next to her, his head lolling against her shoulder. Irritated, she looked down and was about to shove him away when she caught the look of tranquility on his small, dirty face. Like air exhaling from a balloon, anger drained from her and she let him use her as a pillow as he slept. At least he was warm. She was about to ask Ammo Mazen how much longer they were going to be, when he raised his hand in warning. She peered through a gap between the drums. From up the street shuffled a stooped figure. A lantern hung from his hand. As he neared, Nadia glimpsed shaggy white hair, a sharp nose, and a lumpy hand-knit sweater. Footsteps slowed as the man reached the spot where they hid. As if out for a nightly stroll, he stood and casually recited: "'In captivity, a lover suffers in disgrace. And tears flood down his lonely face. In Byzantine land, his body must reside.'"

He paused, as if having forgotten the last bit. Nadia recognized the words right away. It was one of Nana's favorite poems, one she'd made all the boys memorize so that they would have some culture. Even though she wasn't a particular fan of poetry, unless sung to music, even Nadia appreciated the words of Abu Firas al-Hamdani, one of the greatest Arab poets of the tenth century.

To her surprise, Ammo Mazen slowly stood and responded, "'Though in Syrian land his heart does still abide. A lonesome stranger and out of place!

Where none with love may him embrace.'"

"Mazen, is that you?" asked the man, holding up the lantern to see more clearly.

"*Salaam*, Brother Rasheed, yes, it is," replied Ammo Mazen.

"Wonderful to see you," said the man, looking a little startled when Basel popped up, awake now, followed by Nadia. She saw that he had black patch covering his left eye. "But I wasn't expecting you for another week. Is everything all right?"

Ammo Mazen smiled and angled his head toward the kids. "Is there anything truly *all right* anymore?" But it wasn't really a question. "I'm afraid I need to head north, so this will be my last mission."

Nadia gave Ammo Mazen an odd look at the word "mission" and anxiety pooled in her belly. *Is he a spy? Who does he work for? Assad's forces or the rebels?* Her blood ran cold. *Or the mukhabarat?* But that didn't make any sense. He'd been avoiding their cars whenever they'd run across them.

"How is your eye?" asked Ammo Mazen.

"I had hoped to regain my sight, but I'm afraid it's gone. At least I am alive. But forget that—I'm saddened to hear that we will be losing you sooner than we hoped," said Rasheed. "And it's lucky I was still home and spotted your signal from the window."

"A blessing indeed," replied Ammo Mazen.

"All right, then, follow me. Things have changed much since we saw you last. Operations had to be shifted to a more secure location after one of those foreign rebel battalions began to harass us." Rasheed extinguished the candle and led them down a narrow street between the shop with the sign of a tree and a shuttered café.

"I don't know about this," muttered Nadia, pulling her coat tighter.

"It'll be okay," said Basel, giving her a smile as he slipped a piece of charcoal he'd been using to draw into his pocket. He stayed beside her as they darted through a series of streets until they came to a nondescript, low-slung concrete building in a rubbish-filled lot, the shuttered door behind a broken-down truck. Following the men inside, Nadia stilled, inhaling a familiar, sharp metallic scent, a smell she'd recognize anywhere. *Phosphate.* Dug up from mines in the countryside, the mineral had arrived in trucks at her grandfather's factory, where it was made into fertilizer.

If phosphate was not handled properly, it could cause an explosion, her father had warned them during one of his lengthy chemistry lectures. The talk had come soon after her birthday party, when Jad and Malik had gotten into trouble for experimenting with the mineral. Her father had grounded Jad, but had also been impressed by how the boys ingeniously used phosphate to make colorful smoke bombs. Thankfully, Jad and Malik had kept their mouths shut and not named Nadia as a co-conspirator. When she'd caught them watching Internet videos on how to make smoke bombs, she'd blackmailed them into letting her help them, saying if they didn't, she'd tell their parents. Initially ticked off, they'd soon realized how useful she could be: She was the one who got them needed ingredients, like sugar and aluminum foil, from the kitchen. An image of Jad, Malik, and her father flashed in her mind and she clenched her father's cap in her fist. *I have to reach them.*

Rasheed relit his lantern while Ammo Mazen pulled out his flashlight, illuminating a cavernous hall. Nadia squinted into the musty space, looking for the source of the smell. A few ripped bags of fertilizer sat against the wall, where rainwater dripped, forming a pool on the floor. Trailing behind the others, she saw that the room was separated into two sections by a wide arched doorway in the middle.

"You can leave Jamila here," said Rasheed, pointing to a spot beside the doorway. Unlike the other side of the building, this one was crammed to the ceiling with all sorts of odds and ends: towers of old newspaper, bales of hay, wooden boxes, and an assortment of cardboard boxes.

"This way," said Rasheed, pushing aside stacks of folded cardboard. He shuffled toward a tall wooden crate leaning against the left corner.

"Where are we going?" Basel whispered to Nadia. Nadia shrugged, feeling as confused as he did.

At the crate, Rasheed pulled aside the front panel. Behind where it had been, a set of stone steps descended into darkness.

"Wow," whispered Basel, eyes wide. "It's a secret hideout, like the one in 'Ali Baba and the Forty Thieves.'"

"Watch your step," cautioned Rasheed, starting down.

Nadia stared into the darkness, and her heart began to race.

"Don't worry," Ammo Mazen whispered. "We'll only be here a little while."

Nadia nodded, and grudgingly followed Basel, who loped down the stairs, his curiosity sparked. Ammo Mazen paused a moment to shift back the wooden panel behind himself and then followed. Past the last step, Nadia found herself standing on an uneven concrete floor. Before her was a wide hall lined with metal doors. Rasheed shuffled ahead of them, stopping at the last one. He peered back, making sure they were all together, before pushing open the door.

Open sesame, Nadia thought wryly, as warm air and the cacophony of voices rushed from the room.

Chapter Eighteen

October 11, 2013 12:03 a.m.

"Come in, come in," said Rasheed.

Nadia stumbled in beside Basel, Ammo Mazen behind them. Light sparkled from the ceiling, powered by a small generator humming in a corner. People rushed to and fro carrying boxes and bags, or sat hunkered over a line of tables that stretched the length of the room. A group of dusty statues with missing heads, arms, and legs stood in one section, paintings in another, stacked carefully.

"Pretty," muttered Basel, bringing Nadia's attention to a three-legged bronze stag he was examining. Propped next to it lay a jewel-toned mosaic of a man wearing a laurel wreath on his dark curls. Basel moved to take a closer look at how the small glass tiles had been cleverly put together to create the lifelike image.

"Rasheed, I thought you were staying home

tonight," called a birdlike woman with silver hair, hurrying toward them. "Brother Mazen, *salaam*, what a wonderful surprise!"

"*Walaikum assalaam*, Sister Laila," said Ammo Mazen with a weary smile.

"You have lost weight since we saw you last," she said, examining him with concern. "Have you . . ."

Ammo Mazen gently cut in. "Yes, I have. Food is scarce after all, and there is so much work to be done."

"Yes, yes, you are right," said Laila, a frown on her lips.

"It was lucky indeed that your husband was home and brought us to your new location," said Ammo Mazen, smiling.

"We had to move," sighed Laila. "We learned from sources that the old location was to be raided. Months of work would have been lost."

Ammo Mazen's face darkened. "Thugs, our country has been overrun by ruthless thugs. From every side."

"Yes, sadly, I must agree with you," said Laila, turning toward Nadia and Basel. "And who are these young guests?" she asked.

"As we know, life moves in mysterious ways," replied Ammo Mazen. "This is Nadia and Basel, and they have been put in my care. And in turn they have been a great help to me."

Laila winked. "You are lucky you found our ever-resourceful brother Mazen."

Nadia glanced at the old man, wondering again who he was. She also felt a tinge of resentment for having been used as a shield back at the checkpoint. *At least it worked,* she conceded grudgingly.

"What is this place?" Basel burst out.

Laila laughed, eyeing his fatigues. "My young soldier, this is the place where we are fighting a great battle. Our network of helpers collects historical treasures so that we can protect them before they can be destroyed, stolen, or carted off to be sold on the black market."

"This," said Ammo Mazen, great affection in his voice, "is Professor Laila Safi. She ran the archaeology department at the university and is now leading a heroic effort to preserve our history."

"And I am her assistant and husband," said Rasheed, smiling.

"Assistant indeed," admonished Laila. "You are

the proprietor of the most successful bookstore in the city."

"Those days are past," sighed Rasheed. "The bookshop is gone."

"*Insha'Allah*, God willing, they will come again," said Laila, squeezing his hand. She turned to Ammo Mazen, her face grave. "I've heard news that forty percent of the city's ancient landmarks have been damaged or destroyed since the war began."

Forty percent? thought Nadia, shocked. *That's nearly half!*

"Most of the museums in the country, and all six of Syria's World Heritage sites, have been affected in one way or another," she continued. "It makes the work we are doing all the more important."

"The one blessing in this catastrophe is that the mutual love for our history and art has both sides of the war working together," said Rasheed. "We just learned that rebel-friendly archaeologists and the locals of Idlib brokered an agreement with the army to put valuable artifacts behind a thick layer of concrete in the local museum, sealing it off."

"Good news indeed," Ammo Mazen said, nodding.

"Were you able to get the items we were after?" Laila asked.

"Yes, my contact in the Syrian army told me where to recover most of them," replied Ammo Mazen. "Except for the Aramaic scrolls. They were taken by thieves before I could get ahold of them."

Nadia stared at him in surprise. *Contact in the Syrian army?*

"That is too bad," sighed Laila.

"Everything else is in the cart. With some help, I can fetch them," said Ammo Mazen.

"Jamal," Laila called out to a bearded young man packing up a crate with hay. "Please help Sir Mazen."

"I'll be gone a few minutes," Ammo Mazen whispered to Nadia before leaving.

"How is Ilyas?" Rasheed asked his wife as he moved toward a large cardboard box sitting a few feet away. The box, Nadia noticed with surprise, was swaying from side to side.

Laila shared a worried look with her husband. "He's okay as long as he's in there with his books."

Nadia inched closer, Basel at her heels. Suddenly, the box began to shake.

"Would you like something to eat?" asked Laila, bending over the box.

A dark head popped up, accompanied by a loud "No."

It was a boy, Nadia realized, older than her, maybe fourteen. She caught sight of curly hair, tanned cheeks, and round, dark eyes. The head disappeared when a book came up to hide it. It was a copy of Shakespeare's *Macbeth*. "'Her husband's to Aleppo gone, master o' th' Tiger,'" he kept repeating, over and over again.

"Is he okay?" asked Basel.

"Yes, dear," said Laila. "This is our grandson. He has had a very rough time of it since the war started. He doesn't like loud noises and interruptions to his routine, which are now common with the war. Being in the box with his books makes him feel better."

As the professor turned to speak with her husband, Nadia pulled Basel back, wanting to give them some privacy. Finally, she let Mishmish out of his bag so he could stretch his legs. A girl, barely a teen, gave them a smile as she passed, carrying stacked old newspapers to a table. Basel grabbed Nadia's hand and pulled her down an aisle. She was just as fascinated by the activity around them as he was. They paused at a table to watch a woman in a paisley scarf open an old shoe box with gloved hands. Beneath strips of newspaper inside lay a reddish-brown rock. The woman's eyes widened and she pushed aside the remaining paper. *"Ya Allah!"* she cried, causing a lull in the steady hum in the room.

"What is it?" asked Laila, hurrying over.

"I think . . . I think it's one of the Ebla tablets," she whispered.

Ebla, thought Nadia. She'd seen them before, at the National Museum of Aleppo, while on a field trip with her class.

"You're right," said Laila, as others piled around.

"Priceless," whispered a bespectacled man with thinning gray hair.

"It looks like a piece of dried dirt," muttered Basel, elbowing through to peer at it more closely. "Why's it so special?" Nadia poked him in the back, mortified by his rudeness. "Ow," he muttered.

"A very good question," said Laila with a smile. "This tablet, one of thousands, was found in the ancient city of Ebla, just south of here. The Sumerian text provides evidence that nearly five thousand years ago, a rich civilization flourished here, perhaps the *first* recorded world power, equal to that of Egypt or Mesopotamia."

"But these were housed in the National Museum near the Old City," said the woman.

Laila pursed her lips. "Last I heard, the staff at the museum had locked up the building and taken up arms to protect whatever remains. Many items were taken to Damascus for safekeeping . . . but things probably went missing."

Nadia wanted to hear more, but Basel had dragged her to another table, where a woman used a set of tweezers to delicately pluck bits of straw from a strange-looking device that resembled a clock.

"What's that?" Basel asked, staring at its intricate metal designs.

"It's a mariner's astrolabe," she said. "Sailors used it to figure out the positions of the stars and sun, to help navigate at sea."

"Wow," murmured Basel. "Like Sinbad the Sailor."

Nadia rolled her eyes, but the woman laughed. "I'm sure he used one just like this."

As the woman chatted with Basel, Nadia peered

over at a man examining a handful of coins. "Head of Seleucus, general under Alexander the Great, Greek in origin," he muttered, nudging the coin to a corner. "Zenobia, Palmyra's third-century Syrian queen, who revolted against the Roman Empire," he mumbled.

Wow, thought Nadia, squinting down at the next coin and seeing a familiar aquiline profile, stamped in silver. "Salaheddine," she whispered. "It's Salaheddine."

"Very good," said the man, looking up at her. "There is one just like this on display in Room 34 at the British Museum in London. I saw it when I was there many summers ago," he added sadly.

"Is it rare?" asked Nadia.

"Very," said the man, handing it to her. Nadia cradled it in her palm, the cool metal warming as it touched her skin. "Whenever I hold such ancient things, I get the sensation that they have a spirit and a soul. Losing them is like losing a person."

A shiver ran down Nadia's spine as she read the date, "Eleven eighty-four."

"Two years after Salaheddine entered Aleppo, after conquering most of the Middle East," he said. "But unlike our leaders today, who loot, pillage, and kill, he was a true, just ruler. When he drove European Crusaders from the holy city of Jerusalem, he did not kill Christians or Jews. He allowed them to leave peacefully or stay, while preserving their places of worship."

Nadia stared at the image of the warrior king, befuddled by the myriad of emotions rushing through her. She'd heard about the looting of artifacts, but this was the first time she'd seen it firsthand. She had lost so much because of the war: her old life, her family, the luxuries she'd taken for granted. She hadn't thought of what Aleppo, her beloved city, had lost, and was losing. "Can we help?" she asked.

The man grinned. "Of course. We need packaging material." He showed her and Basel how to rip strips of newspaper and crumple them so that they could be used to cushion the artifacts in their boxes.

They'd built up a pile by the time Ammo Mazen returned, perspiration beading his forehead as he carried books from his cart. His bearded young assistant stacked them on a table across from Nadia and Basel. Understanding dawned within Nadia as she examined the book titles: *Kitab al-Tasrif* by medieval Arab surgeon Abulcasis, Katib Chelebi's seventeenth-century Islamic atlas, and other rare books of poetry, history, science, and mathematics. *They're not just old books, they're priceless treasures.* She stared at the old man. *He's not just a book repairer.*

"It breaks my heart," said Rasheed, caressing the cover of a faded volume. "For centuries Aleppo was a center for literature—the first Arabic novel was printed here: *Ghabat al-haqq*, 'The Forest of Truth.'"

"Now, that is an irony," the bearded young man laughed, without humor. "The author, Francis Marrash, wrote about liberty and freedom—both of which Syria lacks."

"Well, does it matter?" muttered Rasheed. "No one reads anymore. All they do is watch those silly soap operas and play games on their phones." Nadia blushed and ducked her head. "Once there was a bookstore on every other street, offering the latest books from Beirut, Cairo, and Damascus."

"And now they've been converted into mobile-phone shops," said the bearded young man, earning a grimace from Rasheed.

"Sadly, you're right," wheezed Ammo Mazen,

before collapsing on a chair, face ashen. From his pocket, he extracted the familiar brown bottle, but when he tipped it over, nothing came out.

About to speak, Rasheed stopped short when he spotted a tall, slim book with gilded edges. "Oh my goodness," he exclaimed. "Is this really *Alef Layla*?"

Startled, Nadia paused in the middle of ripping paper and looked up at them.

Ammo Mazen nodded. "The very one. I believe it's a copy of the fourteenth-century manuscript that Antoine Galland based his French translation on."

"My goodness, this is quite a find," said Rasheed, flipping it open.

"We're lucky you got a hold of these books before they ended up in Jordan, Turkey, or London, sold off to the highest bidder, lost forever," said Laila, joining them, carrying a glass of water for Ammo Mazen.

As the men talked, Nadia eyed the book that had kept her company over the past day, a sense of loss spreading through her. *Don't be stupid. It's just a book,* echoed a mocking voice in her head. Her eyes met Ammo Mazen's and she looked away.

"Where are you taking the kids?" asked Laila.

"The girl to Turkey and the boy to his grandfather," said Ammo Mazen.

"And you are well?" she asked, her voice falling an octave.

"As well as can be with old age and war constantly on our heads," he replied.

Chapter Nineteen

July 19, 2012

A red-stained bandage covered Jad's shoulder. His skin was a pasty gray from all the blood loss. Hand trembling, Nadia wiped her brother's forehead with a cool towel, as she'd been instructed by Khala Lina, to keep his fever down. Her aunt had removed the bullet from his back, and now he battled to keep a life-threatening infection at bay.

"How is he?" her mother whispered from the doorway.

"The painkiller seems to be working," replied Nadia, biting her lip. "He's been out for over four hours."

"I still don't understand how he and Malik ended up at the mosque across town for Friday prayers in the first place," grumbled her mother, for the hundredth time. She stared down at her eldest son. "What were they thinking, getting caught up in that demonstration against the government?"

Nadia stayed silent. She had no answers for her mother, at least none that she could share. It seemed everyone had their secrets these days, and Jad and Malik had been spending an awful lot of time on the computer and having hushed discussions.

"Thank *Allah*, Malik had the sense to carry Jad back home on Jad's motorcycle," mumbled her mother.

Nadia sighed. The events of the last few months, buzzing on the Internet, jostled inside her tired mind. All across the country, government forces and *shabiha* were slaughtering innocent civilians, cleansing Sunni Muslims from Alawite areas. In retaliation, Sunnis were butchering Alawites. Despite the bloodshed in Deraa and other cities, the situation in Aleppo had remained mostly calm, punctuated by sporadic demonstrations. But since February, things had changed. Rebel groups that opposed the Assad regime bombed military and police sites, killing twenty-eight and injuring hundreds of others. Further clashes left large swaths of the countryside under rebel control, while news flooded in of more and more senior Syrian army officials defecting to the rebel side. The number and size of protests had grown. It was at one of these demonstrations that Jad had been shot by Syrian military forces.

Eyes and ears open, picking up news and clues, Nadia realized that the war had changed. She'd seen video clips of horrendous battles where rebels from the Free Syrian Army and the al-Tawhid Brigade, with its many subgroups, fought Assad's forces. Newer clips showed young men with long beards and strange clothes, speaking Arabic in unfamiliar accents, as well as English, French, and Farsi. These were foreigners, flooding into the country, many with extremist religious beliefs, linked with groups such as Al Qaeda and those who called themselves the Islamic State of Iraq and Syria, ISIS, and carried a black flag. As if that weren't complicated enough, money and arms were flooding in from Europe, America, and rich Gulf Arab states to aid Syrian rebels, who were mainly Sunni Muslims. Meanwhile, Iran and Hezbollah forces from Lebanon, who were Shia, flocked to support Assad, as did Russia, which sent military aid. Christians and other minorities were caught in the middle.

"You should eat something," said her mother, interrupting Nadia's thoughts. "Nana made a pot of soup. It's on the stove."

Nadia wearily handed her mother the towel and slipped into the hallway, catching the scent of cumin and cinnamon bubbling away with something meaty. As she neared the kitchen, a heavy thud echoed in the distance, followed by a shake. Startled, she grabbed onto a chair and looked out the sitting room window. It was well past nine o'clock in the evening, and the sun had disappeared long ago. But now a ball of orange blazed in the distance.

"Nadia." She heard her mother running up the hall toward her. Her father followed, a look of fear on his face as the staccato burst of machine-gun fire sounded nearby.

"Cover the windows!" he cried, as the entire apartment complex erupted in commotion.

Nadia huddled beside her bedroom window, watching the flickering lights of fires still burning at the edge of Salaheddine. Word on the street was that rebel troops had taken control of the district and set up checkpoints. A small candle flickered in a window down the street, in an apartment building she'd visited days before. With a heavy heart, she'd watched Ms. Hussain, her music teacher, and her family frantically load suitcases into their car after her last singing class. They were leaving for Amman, Jordan, to stay with relatives until the situation in Aleppo improved. There would be no more music lessons to take Nadia's mind off what was happening around her.

The fire Mohamed Bouazizi had ignited to protest the mistreatment by Tunisian authorities had leapt from one country to the next, across the Middle East. Throwing off the shackles of fear, people rose up with demands for *aysh, hurriya, karama, adala ijtima'ia*—bread, freedom, dignity, and social justice—and began a revolution. Now that fire had ignited Aleppo.

Chapter Twenty

October 11, 2013 2:44 a.m.

An hour after their departure from Professor Laila's hideout, the small group zigzagged through the streets, heading east, avoiding checkpoints. Finally, they paused to rest at the quiet intersection of Zoher and Hafez Streets when Basel insisted he needed to go to the bathroom. Even Mishmish lay slumped in his favorite spot on the cart, behind Jamila's tail. The donkey snorted, shaking her head in a huff, as she and Nadia eyed each other in weary understanding. Nadia collapsed onto the curb, staring down at her tattered shoes and dusty jeans. She pulled off her visor, thinking she'd never been so dirty and exhausted in all her life. *One more stop,* she thought with a frown. *Ammo Mazen promised we'll head north to Turkey after a final errand.* And like last time, he hadn't told them much about where they were going, just that they needed to meet someone in Jdeideh Quarter. The fact that he was so secretive was beyond irritating, and left her a little nervous. The old man had proven that he was far more than a book repairer, and she was trying to be patient, which wasn't exactly her strong suit.

Laila and Rasheed had tried to get them to stay the night, insisting that Ammo Mazen needed to rest, but he'd refused. Nadia was relieved. With hugs and good wishes, they'd left. Professor Laila's group, Nadia realized, no matter how dedicated and hardworking, was but a buoy bobbing in a tidal wave of destruction. *Can saving a clay tablet, some books, and coins really preserve five thousand years of history and culture?* She gazed at the nondescript multistory building standing on the opposite side of the street and couldn't help but feel hopeless.

"That was the Italian consulate," said Ammo Mazen, eyeing the building Nadia was blankly staring at. "The Italians left as soon as the fighting began. The Americans, Canadians, British, French—all gone."

Basel's face darkened as he returned from going to the bathroom. "Stinking French," he muttered.

"What do you know about the French?" asked

Ammo Mazen, amused by the boy's fierce expression.

"My grandfather told me stories, sir," said Basel, puffing out his chest. "*His* father was the leader of our village. The French tried to steal their land when they refused to pay their stupid taxes, so he led an epic battle against them. They still talk about it."

The echo of a long-ago lesson from her history teacher popped into Nadia's head. "It was the British, too," she muttered. "After the Allied Powers defeated the Ottomans and Germans in World War One, they carved up Arab lands for themselves."

"Looks like they're teaching kids *something* useful in school these days," said Ammo Mazen, a twinkle in his eye.

Stung that he thought she didn't know much, the lesson came tumbling from her mouth. "It was called the Sykes-Picot Agreement," she muttered. "Britain took Palestine, Transjordan, and Iraq so they could connect to their empire in India. Greater Syria and Lebanon went to France."

"The French stole Lebanon, too?" squeaked Basel, outraged.

"Yes," said Ammo Mazen. "And to control the

people whose land they occupied, they sowed seeds of division among them. Originally they wanted to create an Alawite, Sunni, Druze, and Christian state. But in the end, they created six—Jabal Druze, Aleppo, Alawite, Damascus, Alexandretta, and Greater Lebanon."

As Basel asked Ammo Mazen how the French were able to maintain power, Nadia couldn't help but compare them to the Alawites, who also kept the majority of Muslims and Christians under their thumb. "Things would have been different if Faisal had become a *true* king," she mumbled, remembering the Arab leader who'd brought Sunni and Shias together. He'd fought with the Allied Powers, hoping to create an independent Arab state.

Ammo Mazen shook his head in irritation, cheeks flushed. "They played Faisal for a fool, allowing him to be a puppet king—a lion without teeth. In the end, France and Britain did what benefited them." He took a raspy breath and pulled out his handkerchief, suddenly overtaken by a fit of coughing.

"Are you okay, sir?" asked Basel as he helped Ammo Mazen sit on the back of the cart.

The old man cleared his throat. "Tired lungs, my

boy," he said, taking a sip of water from a plastic bottle Nadia handed him.

Basel was about to ask something when a few blocks up Nadia saw a set of headlights cruise by. A Mercedes. *Is it the same one we saw earlier?* Fear flared through her.

Ammo Mazen rose from the back of the cart, eyes narrowed behind his spectacles. "Come, children," he said urgently. He grabbed Jamila's reins and hobbled past the consulate into a narrow alley.

They detoured north toward Gare de Bagdad, the deserted train station, and cut across the train tracks. Nadia eyed the ghostly blue-and-white carriages standing idle on the tracks, and a derailed engine. She remembered riding in a similar carriage, watching the countryside flash by, and shelling salty-sweet pistachios from the trip to Damascus she'd just taken with her family. She'd been eight. *Oh, how I would give anything to be back with them again.*

Ammo Mazen, his breathing heavy, slowed upon turning onto a wide, tree-lined avenue, distinctive with its mix of European and Middle Eastern architecture. Missiles and bombs, unimpressed by the upscale apartment blocks and villas, had wrought their damage here as they had on the rest of the city. As the group turned left at the next intersection, heading north, bright lights and the sound of pulsating music startled them. A string of cafés were filled with well-dressed young people drinking coffee and smoking *shisha*; the sweet smell of apple-scented smoke filtered down the street toward them.

"Where are we?" asked Nadia in amazement.

"Aziziyeh," said Ammo Mazen.

Aziziyeh, thought Nadia. An affluent suburb in the northwest of the city. A few young men hovered on ladders, connecting a generator to wires strung with brightly colored lights. They were acting as if they didn't even know a war raged around them.

"Do you think they have something to eat?" Basel muttered longingly.

Ammo Mazen eyed the throngs and shook his head, his face pallid and lined.

"Wait," said Nadia desperately. "Maybe they have a working telephone. I can call my father."

"No," said Ammo Mazen, moving on, but more slowly this time, wincing as if he were in pain. "It's not safe."

"But . . . ," began Nadia, but he'd already turned away, leaving her feeling angry.

"Ammo is right," said Basel, reaching over to squeeze her hand. "Something doesn't seem right. . . . It's best to go."

Reluctantly, she followed as a soulful voice floated toward them. *It's Abdul Karim Hamdan.* He'd been a contestant on *Arab Idol* that summer, a local boy. Haunting lyrics wove over them as they headed down the street, piercing her heart anew: *Oh, Aleppo, oh, my country, you are a spring of suffering in my country.*

Coming to the end of a narrow street, Nadia saw something sparkle high above their heads and slowed.

"Wow," whispered Basel, staring at a glittering arrangement of CDs strung between the buildings and spelling out "Art is peace." Wondering who had risked their life to spend hours creating the display, Nadia hurried to catch up with the cart, dragging Basel with her.

As they turned the corner, they heard the screech of tires and saw a car barreling toward them. It stopped, angled sideways, blocking the street. It was a Mercedes. Like the one they'd slipped past hours earlier.

"You two," whispered Ammo Mazen. "Get behind

the cart." He reached under the tarp to open the secret compartment. From within its depths, he extracted something. *Something metallic.*

A gun . . . it's a gun, thought Nadia, heart racing. She shared a panicked look with Basel as Ammo tucked the weapon into the back of his waistband.

The driver-side window rolled down, revealing a burly, thick-set man with a craggy face. "*Salaam*, Brother Ahmed, I've been looking all over town for you!"

Nadia frowned. *Who's Ahmed?* She glanced at Ammo Mazen. A relieved smile had replaced the look of apprehension. "*Walaikum assalaam*, Brother Sulaiman," he said. "Unfortunately, I haven't had a chance to swing by to see you."

Sulaiman got out of the car and came toward them, his heavy leather jacket hanging loosely above his khaki pants. "Who're the kids?" Sulaiman asked suspiciously.

"Don't worry about them," said Ammo Mazen. "They have their uses."

What does that mean? thought Nadia with a frown.

"Brother Ahmed, I'm in a tight spot," said Sulaiman, his tone weary. "My commander's been breathing down my neck all week. He wants the information you promised me."

"I'm sorry, Brother Sulaiman," said Ammo Mazen, extracting an envelope from inside the secret compartment, along with a bar of gold from the black bag. "It took a while to pinpoint the location of the men you're looking for. They've moved their command post deeper into Salaheddine."

Nadia looked from one man to the other. *Why is Ammo Mazen giving information on rebels to someone from the* mukhabarat*?*

"Thank you. This is *very* helpful," said Sulaiman. He slipped the envelope and gold into his inside jacket pocket. "This will make my commander and his team happy; just enough information to go in search of the rebels, but not enough to actually find them. It will keep them busy for a while."

Nadia was even more confused.

"Yes, it's a tricky dance we perform," said Ammo Mazen, exhaustion lining his face.

"Indeed it is," said Sulaiman, giving him a conspiratorial wink.

"Thank you for the tip on the location of the rare

manuscripts last month," said Ammo Mazen. "We were able to save them."

"That is wonderful," said Sulaiman, checking his watch. "I must go, but I wanted to tell you to be careful, brother. Rumors are floating about, of an old man causing trouble, poking his nose where it doesn't belong. Those higher up have given orders to find you."

"Thank you for the warning," said Ammo Mazen, exchanging good-byes before parting.

Chapter Twenty-One

October 11, 2013 4:07 a.m.

A metal bell lay dented and cracked on the cobblestone path. It had hung in a tower of a building that had collapsed, the victim of a bomb. Nadia glanced at the shattered blocks of sandstone, a hollow feeling spreading through her as she spotted a cross still dangling from the far wall. A look of disgust and anger flashed over Ammo Mazen's face before he turned. They had crossed into Jdeideh, or "New Quarter." It was a strange name, really, since the district had sprung up nearly five hundred years ago to accommodate the growing Armenian community. But compared with the Old City, which lay further east and had been inhabited since the time of the Ebla tablets, it was new. Nadia glumly remembered the last time she'd been here, during a particularly hot summer. After picking her up from school one day, her father had been in a rush to attend one of his boring business meetings. To make up for dragging her along, he promised her a treat. On the way home, they stopped at a famous shop known for *haytaliyeh*—a pudding served with clotted ice cream and orange blossom syrup. The sweet memory of sitting with her father at a small table overlooking the sunny patio faded as she hurried to catch up with the others.

"It looks like a setting from one of Scheherazade's stories," murmured Basel in wonder, craning his neck up and down as they traveled through the confusing warren of narrow alleys, some barely wide enough for the cart.

Indeed, entering Jdeideh was like stepping back in time. Lanterns hung from the walls. Once they would have lit the path, illuminating historic homes and mansions secreted behind heavy stone walls and wooden doors. Now all they could see was dark, gabled first-floor windows, balconies, and unruly bushes and vines trying to escape from private courtyards. Then, without warning, Basel darted through an open door on the left.

"What's the boy up to?" muttered Ammo Mazen, slumped against Jamila, his face ashen and covered in perspiration.

"Are you all right?" asked Nadia, examining his haggard appearance.

"I'll be better once I've made my delivery and had a cup of tea," he said with a forced smile, pointing east. "It's a short distance away from here, past the square."

Nadia nodded. "I'll get him," she said. Passing through the door, she found herself in the inner courtyard of an elegant home. She could see that much of the contents of the house had been carried off, either by its owners or by looters. Past a fountain grew a garden, heady with the scent of jasmine. "Basel, come back this minute," she hissed.

His small head popped up from between two trees, thick with shiny dark leaves. "Look," he said, holding up something round on his palm.

Nadia crept closer and caught the familiar scent of figs. Sharing a grin, they filled a discarded plastic bag with as much of the plump green fruit as they could carry. As they left the house, Basel spotted a stunted tree, surrounded by overgrown vines. From a drooping branch hung a single perfect lemon, which he plucked and tucked away in his pack.

Nadia paused within the doorway, excited to share

a fig with Ammo Mazen. But he was gone. Only Jamila and the cart stood in lane. She peered back up the lane they'd come down. "Where is he?" she gasped, as Jamila brayed in distress.

Basel ran toward the cart. "Here!" he cried.

Near Jamila's front hooves, Nadia glimpsed a hand. "Oh no," she cried, running over and finding the old man lying on the ground, blood oozing from a cut on his forehead. She pushed away the donkey's head to put her ear to his chest, and heard a steady rhythm of a beating heart. "He's alive, girl," she said, petting the worried animal. "Ammo," she asked, "can you hear me?"

Ammo Mazen's eyelids fluttered open. "What happened?" he asked, confused.

"You fell," said Nadia.

He tried to push himself up, but couldn't. "I have to go," he said, voice growing fainter.

"Uncle," said Basel, fetching the water bottle. "Please, you have to take it easy."

"The package . . . the one Alaa gave me," whispered Ammo Mazen. "Get it. It's for the bishop, I gave him my word I would find it."

Nadia retrieved the package, but as she knelt by his

side, he fell unconscious again. "Ammo, please wake up," she whispered, shaking his shoulder.

"What's wrong with him?" asked Basel, clutching the bag of figs.

Nadia sat trembling, drowning in a sea of worry and fear. She was lost in the middle of a city at war, with a mysterious, sick old man whom she trusted one minute and questioned the next. She glanced at Basel, who wanted to fight with the rebels and would probably get himself killed. She screwed her eyes shut, wanting to make everything disappear. *This is too much . . .*, she thought, overwhelmed with panic. *Why is this happening to me? I should just ditch them and go find my family on my own. It would be easier and faster. . . .* She clutched the silver pin so hard it cut into her hand.

"What do we do?" Basel whispered as his skinny arms encircled her in a hug.

The warmth of his body punctured through her riotous emotions. Reflexively, she hugged him back, eyes opening. *Get ahold of yourself . . .*, came a voice inside her head.

I can't leave them behind, she thought. She stared down at the writing on the package. It was the address of a church. Ammo Mazen's last errand. He'd given his word to the bishop—as he'd given it to her, to find her family. He had helped her when she needed it the most. And now she would help him. For now, the questions she had didn't matter. She would trust him.

She rose, filled with resolve. "Come," she said to Basel, kissing him on a wet cheek. "It'll be okay. We need to find the bishop. I'm sure he can help us."

Compass in one hand, Jamila's reins in the other, Nadia strode east, the responsibility of leading their group heavy upon her shoulders. Praying that Ammo Mazen, cocooned within the cart, was all right, she hurried down a sloped street, past a resplendent domed mansion situated at the edge of a square. Jamila halted obediently while Nadia used the mirror stick to peer around a corner. The square sat silent, lined with shuttered cafés, restaurants, and antique shops. About to continue, she froze. A group of armed men had come into view, carrying boxes and packages. The one in the lead, beard neatly trimmed, in flowing dark robes, urged his companions to hurry. Once they'd disappeared into an alley, Nadia scooped Mishmish from his perch behind

Jamila and slipped him into his sack. Irritated at being cooped up, he sank his claws into her wrist. Oblivious to the pain, she set the cat next to Ammo Mazen, who lay on the back of the cart, still unconscious.

From the middle of the square, the silhouette of an iconic bell tower rose against the full moon. Nadia recognized it at once; its picture flashed on television practically every day. It was one of the oldest churches in Aleppo, the Forty Martyrs Cathedral, a spiritual home for the city's Armenian Christians since the fifteenth century. Since the day Jesus arrived in Syria to heal the sick and spread the word of *Allah*, his followers had worked hard to increase the city's prestige and wealth. *It should be nearby,* she thought as they approached the compound that housed the cathedral.

A group of armed men materialized from the shadows. Nadia swallowed, lips dry, and stopped. "Brothers," she called out, wincing at the waver in her voice as she held up the package toward them. "I'm looking for this address. Can you please help?"

A middle-aged man, his worn face not unkind, stepped forward. "It's just down the street, past the Catholic church," he said.

Thanking them, they hurried on, past the Greek Orthodox and Maronite churches, until they reached the Catholic one. Past it rose the destination they sought; a square sandstone building with a trio of heavily armed men guarding the main doors.

"What is your business here?" bellowed a thickset man in jeans and a sweater.

"We need to see the bishop," said Nadia.

"What is your business with the bishop?" said the man, frowning.

"We have something for him, something important," said Nadia. "And our grandfather, he needs help."

The man looked at Ammo Mazen, lying in the back of the cart. With a curt nod, he sent in one of his buddies with the message.

Minutes later, the door burst open, revealing a man in black robes, a long, gray-streaked beard reaching his chest and entangled in a large gold cross, which hung from a heavy chain. He took one look at Ammo Mazen and paled. "What happened?"

"He fell and hit his head," said Nadia. "We need your help."

"My dear child, what is your name?" he asked.

"Nadia," she said, not wanting to reveal more. "And this is Basel."

"I am Bishop Aphrem," he said. "Mazen is a good friend and you are all welcome here."

Relief flooded through Nadia. Two men carried Ammo Mazen inside, leaving Jamila and the cart under the protection of the other guards. She grabbed the package and followed them inside. Soft light from lanterns illuminated a sprawling vaulted space. The marble floor, she was surprised to see, was lined on both sides with bodies covered in blankets. Sounds of sleep echoed through the room. Wooden benches had been moved to the side to make space. The bishop led the men up the central aisle toward the altar built of shining white stone, decorated with gold leaf. From the corner of her eye, Nadia spotted a boy slumped on a bench. Above him rose a statue of the Virgin Mary, her head covered by a veil. Eyes solemn, filled with love, she stared down at the baby in her arms, her son, the prophet Jesus. As Nadia looked at the back of the boy's head, she caught a flicker of red and white. *I know who that is!*

Chapter Twenty-Two

October 11, 2013 4:39 a.m.

Nadia hurried toward the boy as if a *jinni* had taken hold of her body. "It's you," she whispered, heart hammering against her ribs.

The boy awoke, startled, and used his worn red-and-white-checked scarf to wipe wet cheeks. "Yes, it's me," he said with a watery smile.

"Are you okay, sir?" asked Basel, running to catch up with her, his eyes wide with surprise. He still lugged the bag of figs.

"Yes, I'm fine," said Tarek, though there was a cut on his chin and his clothes were torn and dusty.

"You decided to come," said Nadia, brimming with relief.

Tarek's smile faltered and he glanced back at the prophet Jesus, eyes grave. After a moment, he whispered, "*He* was his mother's only son, a miracle from

Allah." Then his face hardened. "*She's* not coming back. There was no use in staying."

Nadia's heart felt heavy. She wasn't particularly good at sympathy. "I'm so sorry," she said simply. She looked at Tarek and could see a well of anguish, a sense of loss that surpassed her own thousandfold. After all, she was on her way to Turkey to find her family. He had given up hope of ever seeing his mother again. She was about to ask how he'd found them, when the bishop called out to them softly.

"I see you've found your friend," he said, accompanying the men carrying Ammo Mazen. "Now all of you, come along with me." He led them toward an arched door a dozen feet down from the altar.

"What happened to Ammo Mazen?" whispered Tarek as the men went first, entering a wide hall that traveled deeper into the church.

"He just collapsed," said Nadia, the excitement of finding Tarek fading. Worry ate at her as she watched the men disappear into a room on the right.

Nadia followed and found a group of men huddled over Ammo Mazen, who was lying on a sofa in a cozy sitting room. To her surprise, she saw the dark-robed figure from the square at the far end of the rectangular room, stacking boxes with his men.

"Give him air," ordered a short man with reddish hair, authoritatively pulling a stethoscope from his bag. As he listened to Ammo Mazen's chest, the bishop leaned over to talk to him. The doctor blinked in surprise, then turned to the dark-robed figure. "Imam Ismail, any medical supplies in those boxes from our Kurdish friends?"

"Yes, there's an assortment of medical instruments, bandages, and medicines."

"Give me glucose," said the doctor. "Also, please show me all the medications you have."

Nadia pushed her way through the men. "Is he okay? What's wrong with him?"

At her voice, Ammo Mazen stirred. "What . . . where am I?" he mumbled.

"Praise be to *Allah*," cried Bishop Aphrem. "You're awake."

"Here, drink this," said the doctor, giving him a cup of water mixed with glucose, plus two pills from a dark bottle in one of the boxes.

After drinking it down, Ammo Mazen sat up, color returning to his cheeks.

"You will need to take these with more frequency," said the doctor, handing Ammo Mazen the bottle, an uneasy look on his face. "Plus, after that skull cracking, you're going to have quite a headache, to be sure."

"Thank you, Doctor," said Ammo Mazen, giving a nod and pocketing the bottle. "These will be a great help indeed." He turned toward Nadia and spotted Tarek. "How did *you* get here?"

"I saw the address written on the package when I picked it up at the mosque," said Tarek with a smile. "You mentioned you needed to drop it off before heading north, so I decided to take a chance."

"Clever boy," said Ammo Mazen, then blinked. "The package!"

"Here it is," said Nadia, holding it out to him.

"Give it to the bishop," said Ammo Mazen, eyes filled with relief. "You're the one who brought it this far."

All eyes on him, the bishop gently peeled away the brown paper, revealing a folio of delicate vellum, the text in faded ink and decorated with gold-and-jewel-toned illustrations. Basel leaned forward to see, and even Nadia found she was holding her breath. With shaking fingers the bishop traced the letters, as someone whispered in reverence, "*Ya Allah*, the *Peshitta*."

"*Pesha* what?" asked Basel.

"This, my child," said the bishop, eyes welling with tears, "is one of the only surviving copies of the original Bible in Syriac, the language closest to what Jesus spoke, which was Aramaic. Where did you locate it, Brother Mazen?"

"It had been taken from the monastery and hidden in a town north of Aleppo," said Ammo Mazen. "My contacts were able to procure it before it disappeared into the black market."

Nadia stared at Ammo Mazen, wondering just how far his web of contacts spread and how he had cultivated them. *Like Sulaiman . . .*

"Thank you," said the bishop, shaking with emotion. He turned to the men. "Brothers, this is Mazen Kader. A dear friend and, as you can see, a procurer of things invaluable."

Ammo Mazen ducked his head, embarrassed. "Now, Bishop, I am no such thing."

"You are a magician," said the bishop, "helping countless with your ingenious ways."

Introductions were made, and it seemed the group represented various churches and social and civic organizations around the city. Given a plate of bread and strips of *basterma*, dried beef, by a young priest, the kids were directed to a corner to sit. Basel handed the priest the bag of figs, which was passed around.

A grizzled old priest took one and stared at it with a forlorn sigh. "It reminds me of the land promised to Prophet Abraham, filled with figs, pomegranates, olives, wheat, and honey—where you could eat without scarcity, and not lack for anything."

His companion snorted. "Now we are in a wasteland where the people starve."

Nadia caught Tarek staring at the rich pink interior of his fig, muttering quietly to himself, "'I swear by the fig and the olive.'"

"Why are you swearing, sir?" asked Basel, chewing with his mouth open. The bread and *basterma* swirled around in a gross mass.

Disgusted, Nadia elbowed him. "Eat with your mouth closed."

"Don't you know anything?" asked Tarek, looking irritated.

Basel shrugged and popped another piece of meat into his mouth.

"There is a verse in the Quran about the fig and the olive," sighed Tarek. "They symbolize the land between Palestine and Syria where such fruits grew, along with the teachings of the prophets Abraham, Moses, Jesus, and Mohammad, peace be upon them."

"Oh," said Basel. "I don't know about symbols, but figs are pretty tasty."

While the boys bickered, reminding Nadia of her brothers, she turned her attention to the men. She glanced at Ammo Mazen with relief. He looked better, but was still very weak. She wanted nothing more than to leave, but watching him sip a soothing broth, she bit her tongue. He needed to regain some strength before they could go.

"Did you hear?" said a pale, slender man as he paced. "The *mukhabarat* sent out leaflets telling people they will face persecution from the rebels. Even though many Christians are in opposition to Assad, others have had close relations with the government, and are scared."

Ammo Mazen nodded. "Fear is understandable.

The *mukhabarat* and the Assad regime use fear to control people, pitting religious groups against each other to keep a hold of his power."

"He's right," said Imam Ismail. "I heard that government workers in the city of Homs were paid to agitate violence. They spray-painted messages all over the city—'Christians to Beirut and Alawites to the grave.' It is driving a wedge between the communities, keeping them from working together."

Just like the French, thought Nadia.

"But if the Assad regime falls, there is talk that opposition groups will take revenge," continued the man. "Especially these extremist foreign fighters coming from abroad—they are out to kill Christians!"

Bishop Aphrem broke in: "Now, now, brother, there is no plan to kill Christians just because they are Christian. Bombs and bullets are equally targeting Muslims and Christians."

"Bishop Aphrem is right," said the grizzled old priest. "Before the war, Syrians of all religions lived in peace for hundreds of years. Now we must come together and fight for peace."

Ammo Mazen put down his cup. "You are both correct. We must battle tyranny, not only from the Assad regime, but also from outsiders who are bringing intolerance toward Christians and toward Muslims who do not believe as they do."

"Brothers, I must go," said the imam. "I must make a delivery to the Jesuit Refugee Service, and there's news that Assad's forces have locked down the area north of Jdeideh."

That doesn't sound good, thought Nadia.

"So there's no passage north from here?" asked Ammo Mazen with a frown.

Nadia's heart sank.

"No, I'm afraid not," said the imam.

"We have to go north," burst out Nadia, unable to restrain her panic.

The men looked at her with a mixture of pity and irritation.

"Yes, my child," said the bishop. "But the path north is perilous from here."

"You will have to go further east, then head north at a safer crossing point," said the imam.

Ammo Mazen looked at Basel. "Well, now we can find your grandfather and the Freedom Army he belongs to."

Basel ducked his head, nodding, while Nadia fumed. *More wasted time.*

Chapter Twenty-Three

October 11, 2013 1:12 p.m.

H*e isn't here,* Nadia thought, waking with a start. She sat up on the sagging sofa, looking for a hint of marmalade fur. Instead, she bumped into something hard—a book. *Alef Layla.* Memories from the night came flooding back, of leaving the church, despite the bishop's pleas to stay. Ammo Mazen had caught Nadia's fearful gaze and insisted they leave. He had taken them to an old hotel where they could rest before heading east. And upon their arrival, Ammo Mazen had handed her the book and said, "I believe you have need of this more than a dusty old library or museum shelf does." Now she stared at his slight figure. He was sleeping, aided by two pills she'd handed him from a bottle labeled MORPHINE. *Morphine,* what Khala Lina had given her to reduce the pain in her leg after surgery. *What pain is he battling?* she wondered.

She glanced past the dusty curtains through the window, where the sun indicated it was well past noon. *We should get moving. But maybe just an hour more rest,* she thought, giving the old man a final, thoughtful look. Tarek lay sprawled on the floor, snoring softly. Something else was missing. *Basel.* The mound of blankets he'd used to construct a nest was empty. She peered across the run-down sitting room. *Nothing.*

Crossing the threadbare rug, she tiptoed through the door and ran across the black-and-white-tiled foyer to the front door Ammo Mazen had unlocked with his skeleton keys when they'd arrived. *Still locked.* The door to the bathroom stood ajar. She inched along the wall and peered inside. Mishmish snoozed beside Basel, who lay curled up in a tight ball, asleep. At his feet lay his gun. And all around him, on the tiled floor, he'd drawn a picture with a piece of charcoal. It was of an old woman in a dress, stick arms and legs jutting out. In one of the figure's hands was a lemon, like the one he'd plucked from the tree in Jdeideh. *Lemons . . . his grandmother loved lemons.* Propped against the door, Nadia felt grief consume her. *Nana . . . where is she? Where is everybody?* She wanted to reach down and hug the little boy, as if he were her own Yusuf. She wiped the tears away and forced herself to head toward the foyer. She needed to steel herself before waking the others. She was thirsty. She headed past a yellowed advertisement hanging on the wall:

> *Hotel Baron, the only first-class hotel in Aleppo. Central heating throughout, complete comfort, uniquely situated. The only one recommended by travel agencies.*

A faded World War II–era Syrian map hung beside it, along with an old poster announcing a trip aboard the Orient Express, in which one would travel in opulence from Europe to Baghdad via Constantinople, stopping in Aleppo. She spotted an old-fashioned black telephone hanging in a booth. The line was dead, of course, telecommunications still down. With a sigh, she wandered on through the elegant yet shabby hotel, followed by Mishmish. She peered at old photographs and memorabilia displayed on the walls and headed toward the wood-paneled dining room, tiled with green and brown ceramic. Her stomach growled for a hard-boiled egg or just a slice of bread, as an old memory blossomed, of wearing a frilly pink dress, legs dangling from one of these chairs. At a table beside her, her father huddled with men in business suits, haggling over phosphate prices, as a jovial old waiter brought her lemonade. Seeing her glum expression, he entertained her with stories of the prestigious hotel and its illustrious guests. King Faisal had declared Syria's independence while standing on the balcony in Room 215, and presidents from around the world had stayed at the famous Hotel Baron, including Theodore Roosevelt of America, who'd sat in the same room, enjoying roast pheasant, venison stew, Persian caviar, imported French wines, and rich puddings. The first man to travel in space, cosmonaut Yuri Gagarin, had been a guest, and the famous mystery author Agatha Christie had written *Murder on the Orient Express* while sitting on the terrace sipping tea.

Nadia picked up Mishmish and turned toward the front desk, wondering where the kitchen was. As she passed, the cat stiffened in her arms, hissing. A large black terrier sat beside the desk, its head buried in the lap of an unshaven man slumped over in a chair, his eyes closed, navy woolen cap askew. A handful of papers was clutched in his hands. *Dead. He's dead,* she thought, horrified. The terrier's nose twitched, and the dog jerked up with a shattering bark. Mishmish burst from her grasp, leaving painful scratches, and Nadia screamed.

Seconds later, Tarek and Basel stood beside her, while Ammo Mazen hobbled toward them, breathing hard. "Are you all right?" he asked.

The man was not dead, but was staring at Nadia as if she had two heads. "Quiet, Sasha," he said, patting the dog to calm him.

"Armen, is that you?" asked Ammo Mazen, coughing as Tarek held him up. "We didn't mean to frighten you."

The man, Armen, blinked blearily. "No, no, it's all right," he said, patting the dog, who now sat obediently, though Nadia could tell he wanted to track the smell of cat.

"Apologies, but we let ourselves in early this morning," said Ammo Mazen, sitting in the chair Basel had dragged over for him.

"You are always welcome. As you can see, there are quite a few vacancies," said Armen, peering at the old man with a frown. "Mazen, are you all right?"

"'Time is like a sword,'" murmured Ammo Mazen. "'If you do not cut it, it will cut you.' And the sword of time has taken its toll on me these past few months."

Nadia frowned at the old man's cryptic use of the proverb. Armen nodded, eyes troubled as he glanced at the kids.

"How are you, my friend?" asked Ammo Mazen. "And your family?"

Armen sighed, a deep, soulful sound rushing from his lungs. "We are fine, but hold our hearts in our hands, watching the city tear itself apart. I fear the best years are behind us." His eyes glassy, he stared out over the lobby.

"Don't think that way," said Ammo Mazen.

Armen snorted. "My great-grandmother had the idea to build a luxury hotel in Aleppo while on her way to pilgrimage to Jerusalem from Armenia, nearly a hundred years ago. Did you know that?" he asked, not really expecting a reply. "I remember the day Hafez al-Assad came, shortly after his coup. And his son . . . even *he* came here." Deflated by his outburst, Armen seemed to shrink. He added, voice hoarse, "We survived two world wars, multiple deportations, several coups, and thirty-five years of socialism. But I don't know if we'll survive this."

"It will all be well again," consoled Ammo Mazen. "Your family's hotel is part of the very fabric of Aleppo."

Armen nodded, and shrugged off his outburst with a tired smile.

"By the way," added Ammo Mazen, "have you heard of the rebel group the Freedom Army?"

Basel froze, a look of panic on his face. Nadia frowned. *Why isn't he excited about reuniting with his grandfather?* she wondered.

"No, I'm afraid not," said Armen. "The rebel groups are like rabbits, doubling their numbers every month."

Ammo Mazen nodded, shivering as he pulled his coat in tighter. "My friend, I am on my way to Turkey and do not know when I will return."

"Turkey?" asked Armen, surprised.

"Yes, to take these children to safety," said Ammo Mazen.

Armen nodded, then gave him a cryptic look. "I've heard some things . . . ," he murmured, trailing off.

"Children," said Ammo Mazen. "Please get me a glass of water, will you?"

"The kitchen is that way," said Armen, pointing down the hall.

Nadia exchanged a look with Tarek. With Basel in the lead, they walked toward the kitchen, but Nadia lingered around the corner, pretending to tie her shoelace.

"Men dropped by earlier this week, asking about you," said Armen, voice low.

"I was expecting this," said Ammo Mazen. "Someone has recognized me and is asking questions."

"I told them I hadn't seen you in months," said Armen. "You must be careful. I don't know how long you can play on the razor's edge. . . ."

Razor's edge? thought Nadia, hating it when adults spoke in riddles.

"The children have proved useful, particularly at checkpoints," said Ammo Mazen.

Nadia frowned. *Useful? What does that mean?* Doubts she'd buried resurfaced.

"We all have our destiny, written in the stars," continued Ammo Mazen with a sigh. "My journey is soon at an end."

Chapter Twenty-Four

October 11, 2013 3:00 p.m.

"We must be swift, but careful," said Ammo Mazen, weariness lining his face, as he slipped out the front door into the gray of late afternoon. He'd been nearly as eager as Nadia to leave, not waiting for the cover of darkness he usually preferred.

They passed the large vintage thermometer hanging on the wall beside the door, inscribed in French. "It's only nine degrees Celsius," reported Basel.

It sure feels like it, thought Nadia, shivering as she buttoned her coat up to her chin and pulled her father's cap and the protective visor over her head. She watched as the boys helped Ammo Mazen descend the steps to the carport, mistrust clawing at her heart as she recalled his words to Armen. *Is he just using us as cover to navigate through the city? Who is looking for him and why?* She wondered if she should have shared what she'd learned with Tarek. But she had no proof that he meant them harm, and how could he? He was so ill he could barely walk. And so far, all he'd done was help them, and all the other people they'd met. Shrugging off the sensation that something wasn't right, she followed, realizing that she would have to be on her toes, safeguarding the boys while making sure they all got to Turkey.

"The Old City is just a few blocks from here," said Ammo Mazen, looking at each of them in turn, his usually gentle face grim. "It's overrun by different rebel groups, many of them squabbling among themselves. And the citadel is under Syrian army control, with snipers posted along the top. Once we pass it, we'll turn north. If we're stopped, use the same story: I'm your grandfather and we're looking for shelter at a relative's house because ours was bombed. Understood?" They nodded.

Nadia took the reins while slipping the compass into her pocket. "Come on, girl, time to go," she whispered in the donkey's ear.

Jamila stared into her eyes and brayed softly in reply, stepping through the iron gates out onto Baron

Street. Nadia took a deep breath; the air smelled like rain. *Good,* she thought, glaring up at the rooftops with a shiver. On their way to the hotel, they'd heard shots fired at a passing van and realized a sniper sat like a vulture atop the Sheraton hotel. Rain would make seeing through the scope of a rifle more difficult. *I hope the merciless* kalb *drowns. . . .*

"Water," sighed Tarek, rubbing a raindrop across his cheek. "*Allah* tells us he made every living thing from water."

"Really?" asked Basel, and they fell into a whispered theological discussion.

"Stay within the shadows," said Ammo Mazen, keeping an eye on the rooftops as he lay in the cart, watching for any hint of movement. Nadia complied while taking a last look over her shoulder at the once grand Baron Hotel.

At the next corner, a group of men stood huddled beneath the awning of a travel agency, having a hushed, intense conversation.

Nadia slowed, the boys crowding in closer as Ammo Mazen called out, "*Salaam*, brothers. What news is there of the Old City?"

The youngest, the collar of his coat upturned, replied, "Things have been quiet after all the fighting. Perhaps a bit *too* quiet."

"Yes," added his friend, restlessly rocking on the balls of his feet. "It feels like the calm before a storm."

"I'm just tired of it all," grumbled the first. "Life was hard before the war, but good enough. Why did we have to go off and start fighting?"

His friend punched him in the arm, eyes wary. *Keep your thoughts to yourself,* Nadia could hear him think.

"Thank you," replied Ammo Mazen. The men nodded politely and melted into a side street. "Head to the square," he said, coughing, pointing toward the clock tower that rose in the distance. "There is a gate there that leads into the Old City."

"Rest, Ammo," said Tarek, adjusting the pillows and blankets they'd taken from the hotel to make him more comfortable.

"Thank you," said Ammo Mazen with a smile, his voice hoarse. "I think I will close my eyes for a bit."

Jamila, who had a mind of her own, leapt forward, eager to keep moving. Mishmish sat behind her, tied with a leash, nose twitching as he sniffed the wind.

With Nadia in the lead, Tarek and Basel flanked either side of the cart. Spine straight, eyes on the road, Basel was a pint-size soldier on the lookout for trouble. Only Nadia knew what lay beneath the bluster of his tough-guy act.

North . . . Turkey . . . Father . . . , thought Nadia. Her mental recitation was interrupted as the echo of hand grenades was heard in the distance, following by answering machine-gun fire. She calculated it was a quarter of a mile away, in the direction of the Old City. *Not good . . .* She shared a worried glance with Tarek as they crossed the street, which was empty except for a few people hurrying along, carrying supplies and food they'd collected. On the other side of the street, a gray building straddled the block, circled by an iron fence. Hundreds of sandbags lay stacked across the courtyard. Up closer, she realized that they weren't just lumpy sacks; a massive stone foot protruded from beneath. A few yards down from it stood a craggy Roman god, guarding the main entrance of the building, barricaded by concrete blocks. *I've been here,* she thought. It was the National Museum. Professor Laila had told them how the curator and staff had locked themselves inside, trying to protect priceless treasures, like the Ebla tablets.

They soldiered on, moving cautiously as they approached the edge of a square where the city's famous clock tower still stood. Nadia remembered visiting with her family, strolling along Yarmouk Street to their favorite juice vendor. She licked her dry lips as the sweet-tart memory of pomegranate came back. She shook her head of the memory and peered past a broken-down gasoline truck.

"Bab al-Faraj, the Gate of Deliverance," muttered Ammo Mazen, staring at the far side of the tower, where a city gate could be seen, one of the nine original entrances to the Old City. Unfortunately, it was guarded by a dozen men in fatigues, and they didn't look friendly. Abruptly, half of them grabbed their rifles and hurried beyond the gate into the Old City.

"We can't go this way," said Nadia, stomach sinking.

"There's another gate, back the way we came," said Ammo Mazen, pulling out a kerchief to muffle the coughs that shook his body.

He's getting worse, thought Nadia, staring at his pale face. She turned the cart around and they merged onto a parallel street, which took them south, along the old city wall. The street was lined with silent shop fronts, where haggard figures lurked in the rubble, scavenging. Burned-out cars obstructed the path. As they neared a fork in the road, Nadia held up her hand in warning and pulled Jamila to a halt behind the burned-out husk of a truck. She took out Ammo Mazen's stick with the mirror and angled it down the road.

"Let me see," whispered Ammo Mazen, getting off the cart, his steps uneven. "Bab al-Antakya is down another hundred yards. It doesn't appear to be guarded."

The old man climbed back onto the cart with Tarek's help.

As they neared, Nadia could see why the gate had been left unmanned. It was once the western gate into the city, but now it was reduced to rubble, blocking entry. While Nadia and Tarek investigated the damage, Basel wandered up the street, light-footed as a cat, looking for a place to relieve himself.

Nadia hurried over to help Tarek try to shove aside blocks of stone.

"That's no use, children," said Ammo Mazen. "I'm afraid . . .

"Hey," interrupted Basel, waving at them from further down the road. "Over here!"

The explosion that had destroyed the gate had blown a path straight through a workshop next door.

"Watch your step," whispered Tarek, taking the lead as Nadia tugged Jamila's reins, Basel keeping an eye on Ammo Mazen from behind. Inside the ruined shop, it was tricky maneuvering the cart over leather scraps, metal tools, and shattered machinery parts.

As Nadia entered the street on the other side, her foot landed in a puddle of freezing water. Extracting her foot, she saw that the alley was strung with sheets and froze. *Snipers* . . . The rooftops were clear, but from the corner of her eye she caught something stirring at the end of the lane. Something black fluttered, then disappeared into the ruins of a small restaurant, its sign for roast chicken crumpled on the ground. Somewhere in the distance, revolutionary music ebbed and flowed, as if played from a moving car.

"We need to go," urged Basel, holding his rifle close.

Nadia pulled out the compass. "That way," she

said, pointing to a narrow street that veered east.

Carefully, they crept through narrow alleys and natural fortifications provided by the Old City's historic architecture, which had served as cover for both the Syrian army and rebels who had turned the Old City into a battlefield. Elegant, venerable homes; schools; caravansaries, where caravans along the silk route plied their goods; bathhouses; and mosques lay mangled, their innards littering the streets—carved pillars, shattered tiles, furniture, and personal items of those who'd fled.

At the corner, they turned past an Ottoman villa, gutted by mortar, its beams bent and broken. Nadia craned her ears, hunting for echoes of gunfire, but besides the patter of rain, the only other sound came from the lurch and creak of steel and stone, like sinister wind chimes. So focused was she on the compass that she didn't see that the boys were no longer walking beside her.

"Nadia," hissed Basel, "stop. . . ."

She turned and found them standing still, open-mouthed and staring at the horizon. She frowned, wondering why they were examining an empty patch of sky. Then it hit her. "Where did it go?" she blurted. A magnificent minaret had once stood in that spot, a part of the skyline for nearly a thousand years, rising from the Umayyad Mosque. Unlike traditional cylindrical minarets, this one had been square, blush-colored stone, wrapped in intricate Arabic inscriptions. As Nadia gaped, wind rustled past, reminding her of the call to prayer that had flowed from the minaret five times a day, calling believers to prayer from all over the Old City.

"I heard government artillery knocked it down. The dome collapsed into a pancake, destroying Prophet Zechariah's tomb," said Tarek, spitting on the ground as if he had a bad taste in his mouth.

"Wanton destruction . . . ," muttered Ammo Mazen, cheeks pale as he surveyed the damage. "It survived sackings by Abbasids, Byzantines, Armenians, and Mongols—even an earthquake. And its library—priceless manuscripts and books reduced to ashes—I could not save any."

"Come," said Tarek softly. "No point lingering here."

Nadia nodded and slipped into an alley. Handsome

homes, empty of residents, flanked the lane. They were remarkably intact.

It's too quiet, thought Nadia. The hair on the back of her neck was rising.

"Wait," hissed Basel from up ahead.

She and Tarek froze, staring toward a gap between two sagging houses where the boy pointed. Sandbags, piled high, blocked the parallel street. A man stood beneath a balcony, his cigarette glowing in the shadows.

"Turn around," she whispered urgently, tugging on the harness, Jamila's eyes rolling with fear.

Chapter Twenty-Five

October 11, 2013 4:18 p.m.

"Go, go, go!" hissed Basel, grabbing Mishmish and shoving him into his canvas bag for safety.

"I can't. . . . The cart, it's stuck," cried Nadia, tugging on Jamila's reins.

Tarek crawled under the cart to push from behind.

Ammo Mazen slipped down from the back and joined him, face white with exertion, breathing heavily.

Oh, no . . . , thought Nadia, desperate to get away. *Just leave the cart. . . .* Her eyes met Jamila's, which were rolling with fear. *We can't leave her.* She patted the frightened animal's neck, whispering, "It's okay, girl."

"Wait! Stop!" called out a harsh voice.

Footsteps echoed up the alley. "Come on, girl," Nadia urged as the cart creaked forward. But it was too late. A pack of men in civilian clothes blocked their path.

"Who are you?" asked a shaggy-haired figure at the head, his rifle raised.

"My name is Mazen Kader," said Ammo Mazen, coming to the front to shield the kids, shakily holding up his hands. "I'm a bookseller, traveling with my grandchildren."

"What are you doing here?" asked the man, eyes narrowed.

"Our house was destroyed by *barmeela*," continued Ammo Mazen, sagging against Jamila. "We are trying to reach relatives beyond the Old City."

"Brother Khalid," called a voice from the back, "they're just civilians."

Nadia frowned, trying to place the man's accent. The interrogator hesitated, lowering his rifle as a lean figure elbowed his way to the front.

Heart racing, Nadia stared at the young man, dressed in crisp jeans and a thick coat, carrying a camera in a bandaged hand. His dark eyes were shrewd, and a week's worth of stubble grew along his jaw. "They could be helpful," he said to the leader, Khalid, who nodded.

Then he turned to them. "My name is Ayman—I'm a journalist. I'm sorry we frightened you."

"You did," Basel blurted out.

Ayman grinned. "I don't want to inconvenience you, but are you coming from the western side of the city?"

Before Ammo Mazen could reply, Basel piped up. "Yes, from Salaheddine." Nadia elbowed him to be quiet.

"I heard rumors that the army was pushing in from that point," said Ayman. "Do you mind if I ask you a few questions?"

Ammo Mazen looked warily at him and the armed men, and finally nodded.

Twenty minutes later, they were huddled around a fire, juggling mugs of hot, sweet tea and handfuls of almonds while Ammo Mazen provided Ayman with news of Salaheddine, the spate of *barmeela* attacks, and the impending movement of the Syrian army. Nadia eyed Ammo with a pang of worry. Although he'd taken a pill the doctor had given him back at the church, he was drooping in his seat.

"Thank you for agreeing to talk to me," said Ayman, jotting down notes. "I want to tell the outside world what is happening here, share stories of the people and their suffering. The Assad regime has a stranglehold on the news coming out of the country. He's kidnapping, torturing, and killing journalists, but I, and others like me, will not let him hide his crimes."

Ammo Mazen smiled at his earnest expression. "We need people like you to tell the truth of what is happening here. Now, tell us what is happening outside Aleppo."

"The fact is that things are getting worse by the day," said Ayman. "Over a hundred thousand Syrians have perished in the bloodshed and nearly two million have fled the country." Nadia sat back, reeling at the terrible numbers. "Assad has intensified his attacks all over the country and is using more and more deadly force, including chemical weapons."

"We heard about Ghouta," said Ammo Mazen, expression grim as he recalled the city Assad had attacked with poison gas.

"There are rumors that Assad plans to encircle Aleppo and cut rebel supply lines into the city. But it's not just the government," he added, voice falling an octave as he eyed his companions. "Rebel groups, including foreign fighters, are carrying out atrocities against civilians. There are bombings, executions, kidnappings, and torture."

"What is the outside world doing?" asked Tarek, aghast.

Ayman's nostrils flared. "The Americans, Europeans, and others sit at the United Nations bickering, while the Syrian foreign minister pompously tells them that Syria is not engaged in a civil war but a war on terror."

"War on terror," muttered the man who'd made their tea. He had an ugly gash across his forehead. "The only terrorist is Assad!"

A boy, barely in his teens, rose in the back and kicked a metal can, muttering, "No one cares if we die."

"I wish we could offer you more food," said Khalid, "but our supplies are gone."

"Thank you for your hospitality," said Ammo Mazen, "but we know how terrible the situation is."

"It's so bad that clerics have issued a religious edict that it's okay to eat *haram*, or forbidden foods, such as dogs and cats," muttered Tarek. The men looked at the cat in Nadia's lap with revulsion as Nadia angrily elbowed Tarek in the ribs. "Sorry," he whispered apologetically, rubbing Mishmish under his chin.

"We are indeed in dark times," sighed a man, staring into the fire.

"Where are you from?" Basel asked, leaning toward Ayman.

Tarek gave him a rebuking look, but Nadia understood. Ayman's Arabic sounded different, and frankly, his accent was terrible.

"America," Ayman said. "But my family is originally from Egypt."

"Pah, he's a regular pharaoh," joked a man, and Nadia smiled.

The men laughed, a bright, cheerful sound. For a moment they were transformed into what they'd been before the war: farmers, shopkeepers, taxi drivers, and office workers. *They are fathers, brothers, sons, and husbands,* she thought. She ached for her family, her brothers, wondering if her father was waiting for her at the allotted spot at the border.

She shivered, leaning into the fire as rain drizzled in through gaps in the plastic above them. She spotted one of the men pulling out his cell phone.

Hope leapt through her heart. "Does it work?" she asked.

"No, the network's still down," he grumbled, turning it off.

"Be careful with that," said Ayman. "Government forces are using cellular signals to track rebels."

"He's right, you must be careful," said Ammo Mazen, glancing down at his watch. "If you have asked your questions, we must be going."

"You will need to take another path," said Khalid. "The road you were on is blocked by those foreign bastards who call themselves ISIS. They've been fighting other rebel groups to usurp power."

"Shameful," whispered Tarek. "Muslims fighting Muslims."

"Islam has nothing to do with it," said Khalid, a look of disgust on his face. "These foreign hypocrites use religion as an excuse to fight some glorified war, seeking power and fame. They are ruthless barbarians, posting videos on the Internet of their atrocities, like blowing up ancient sites or killing civilians for not following their brand of Islam."

"And we Syrians die, caught between outsiders and Assad," added the man with the gash on his head.

Ammo Mazen shook his head. "I pray you make it safely out of the country, my son," he said to Ayman. "Tell the world about the plight of the Syrian people." As Tarek and Basel helped him settle on the cart, he turned to ask, "Do any of you know where the rebel group the Freedom Army could be?"

Basel froze and ducked behind Nadia. *What's wrong with him?* she thought.

"Freedom Army?" asked Khalid. "Never heard of them."

Ammo Mazen frowned. "Young Basel's grandfather is with them."

The men looked at each other and shrugged.

"Basel," Ammo Mazen called out.

But the boy didn't budge, so Nadia stepped away from him, confused about why he was acting so shy all of a sudden. He stood there, red-faced.

"Basel, what is your grandfather's battalion called?"

"I made it up, sir," he whispered, so softly they had to lean in to hear.

"What?" cried Tarek.

Everyone looked baffled, except Ammo Mazen. "Were both of your grandparents in the building when it was bombed?"

Basel nodded.

Nadia felt as if someone had punched her in the stomach. *He has no family at all.* She lay her arm across the boy's rigid shoulders and held him close without saying a word.

"All right, then," said Ammo Mazen, as if the conversation hadn't taken place. "We must be leaving now."

Basel's hand clutched in hers, Nadia followed a circuitous route northeast, as directed by Khalid. Basel was her responsibility now, whether she liked it or not, as was Ammo Mazen, who lay in the cart with his eyes closed. *He needs to get to a doctor quickly,* she thought. They headed deeper into the Old City. The air grew redolent with the smell of smoke, and an inky residue coated the buildings. Nadia ran her finger along a wall and it came back covered in soot. A memory stirred in her mind, of the previous year, on a cool September night.

Chapter Twenty-Six

September 28, 2012

Nadia and her parents, aunts, uncles, and cousins clustered along the balcony of Nana's apartment, watching in horrified silence as black clouds billowed up from the east, across the river. News quickly made its way through the neighborhood, and Jad brought the latest as he came panting through the balcony doors: The Old City was burning. It was less than four and a half miles away, and they could see the fires illuminating the sky, eating everything in its path like a plague of locusts.

"Ya Allah," Nadia's mother whispered, tears slipping down her cheeks.

"I can't believe it," Khala Lina growled. "They are destroying the very heart of Haleb . . . erasing five thousand years of history and culture."

Nadia's father stood stony-faced. "Father cannot

see this," he muttered. "He will not be able to bear seeing his childhood home like this."

Nadia's mother squeezed his hand. "Don't worry, he's in his room. Your mother is with him."

"The rebels are holding strong against the army," said Jad, cheeks flushed.

"They're both destroying the city," grumbled Khala Lina.

A sick feeling spread through Nadia's middle as she leaned over the railing of the balcony, her small hands held up against the brilliance of the flames. She'd been to the Old City countless times, especially when visitors wanted to tour its rich medieval sites.

A highlight of the day always included shopping at its famous *souq*. Sprawling for miles in all directions, the *souq* was a network of bazaars, the largest covered market in the world. It spanned seven glorious miles and had over six thousand shops. Each *souq* specialized in something unique: Souq al-Hiraj was noted for its rugs and carpets, Souq Khan al-Jumrok sold textiles, and Khan al-Shouneh was a fascinating labyrinth crammed with art, ceramics, and handicrafts. Ladies flocked to Souq as-Siyyagh to purchase gold jewelry and gems, while blacksmiths labored over elaborate metalworks in Souq al-Haddadin. And it was all burning, centuries of history and culture turning into ash. As Nadia stared at the glowing flames, a cold, dreadful certainty blossomed in her heart. She glanced at her father's beloved face from under her eyelashes. Etched upon his features was the terrible knowledge that the world as they knew it had changed and there was no going back.

Chapter Twenty-Seven

October 11, 2013 5:32 p.m.

At the next turn, the winding path deposited them at a wide intersection, and Nadia realized where they were. In the very soul of Aleppo, its ancient *souq*.

Nadia pulled out the compass, which pointed north through the *souq*, as Ammo Mazen sat up, a sheen of perspiration covering his ashen face.

"Are you all right, uncle?" she asked.

"Just tired, my child," he said with a weary smile. "I'll feel much better once we leave the Old City."

"Which way should we go?" she asked, showing him the compass.

"We'll cut through the *souq* here," said Ammo Mazen, pointing to an arched doorway. "Then we'll curve around the citadel to the Bab al-Hadid gate."

Nadia nodded, staring stony-faced at the charred

remains of the shops facing the street. She guided Jamila through one of the main, arched doorways that led inside the *souq*. A sorrowful emptiness ebbed throughout the covered passageways, stone walls cracked and crumbling from mortal shells and grenades.

They merged onto one of the main arteries that ran through the bazaar, lit by skylights embedded in the vaulted ceiling, revealing the extent of the destruction. Nothing much of the *souq*'s rich glory remained, except for hints of its past, strewn on the floor: turquoise shards of pottery, a muddied rug, and torn wisps of bright silk.

Corrugated iron sheets, pockmarked with bullet holes, sealed off sections of the *souq*, and the majority of shops and stalls had been destroyed—shriveled husks of what they had been. But what overwhelmed her most was the silence; it burned like acid through her soul. Her breath caught in her throat. *It's all gone,* she thought. "Why?" she croaked, fists clenched. "Why does *Allah* hate us?"

Tarek stared at her, horrified.

"Nadia," Ammo Mazen said, voice soft. "*Allah* does not hate us. He does not hate anyone."

"Then why is this happening to us?" She waved her arms at the destruction around them.

"True believers," said Tarek, shooting her a pained look, "know that this world is a temporary one. Every day *Allah* tests us with trials and tribulations, small or big, weighing our good and bad deeds."

"Well said, Tarek." Ammo Mazen smiled. "We have been given free will to make choices on how we live our lives, and how we use the blessings given to us."

"Only by choosing good over bad will we reach the final, permanent place," said Tarek.

"That's heaven, right?" whispered Basel, eyes hopeful.

Tarek patted him on the back with a smile.

"Nadia, my child," said Ammo Mazen, muffling his coughs. "Despite *Allah*'s magnificence and majesty, the two qualities most attributed to him are compassion and mercy. And just because those around us are not merciful and compassionate, we should not turn away from following his example."

"And we have been promised that with every hardship there is ease, even with the most difficult trials," added Tarek.

Nadia frowned, chagrined by their words.

"It's in our hands, my dear," said Ammo Mazen. "Always in our hands . . . to choose mercy and compassion, or be lost in a sea of inhumanity."

Not feeling particularly merciful, Nadia grudgingly nodded. She guided Jamila through a central passage where dozens of alleys snaked off, leading to different areas of the *souq*. What shops and stalls fire had not destroyed were shuttered and boarded up. As the passage curved, Jamila hesitated, ears tucked back. Tarek had fallen behind to inspect an alley that branched off to the left, but he suddenly turned, a frown marring his brow.

"What is it?" whispered Basel, rifle raised.

"It's okay, girl," Nadia whispered to the donkey. *Something is spooking her,* she thought, gently rubbing Jamila's neck and looking around for a hint of what it could be.

Tarek held his hand up as something stirred in the silence: the skitter of pebbles along a passage to their right. "We should hurry," he whispered, eyes wide.

"Come on, girl," said Nadia, gritting her teeth as she tugged on Jamila's reins.

Ammo Mazen's eyes flickered open. "Is everything all right?"

"Yes, nothing to worry about," said Tarek, as he and Basel hurried to the front of the cart to help Nadia.

While the boys tried to coax the donkey forward, Nadia untied Mishmish, who sat growling, ears flat against his head. She pried his claws from the tarp and shoved him into his burlap bag. She had just slipped him under a blanket beside Ammo, when they heard gunshots.

"We have to go now," muttered Tarek, voice tight.

"Which way?" gasped Basel as the sound of gunshots grew closer.

The alley Tarek had been inspecting was half filled with rubble, making it difficult for the cart to get through. "The next one," said Nadia, pushing at the cart from behind to nudge the donkey forward.

Basel spoke coaxingly to Jamila, but the donkey wouldn't budge. "Don't be stubborn now," grumbled Tarek as he ran to the front of the cart and pulled.

Ammo Mazen's eyes widened. "Jamila, my dear, please listen to the children," he said, reaching out a shaky hand to rub her back. She turned to the old man and nuzzled his hand, then turned to go, just as a bullet whistled by, embedding itself into the wall.

Nadia fell to the ground with a gasp, barely avoiding another shot. It missed Ammo Mazen by an inch, but grazed Jamila's rump. Braying in pain, she took off down the main passageway, dragging Tarek and Basel along with her as they held on to her harness. Nadia lay there, frozen, as the thud of boots thundered from the lane to her right.

Move, you silly girl! yelled a voice inside her head that sounded like Ms. Darwish. *Do you want to get killed?*

"Am I crazy, or was that the sound of a donkey?" guffawed a youthful voice from around the corner, sending Nadia crawling on her hands and knees.

"Forget that for now," barked an authoritative voice. The footsteps thundered to a halt in the main passageway as Nadia slipped into the mouth of the first alley. "Secure this location. And you, Abu Amir, take a dozen men and head to the citadel to join the others. But be careful of those damned snipers."

Without thinking twice, Nadia rose and scurried up the corridor, scrabbling over rubble, wincing as a slab of concrete scraped her shin. *I have to find the others,* she thought, heart hammering in her chest. At the next intersection, she paused, mentally creating a map, trying to evaluate whether this alley would connect to the one the others had taken. She strained her ears for the sound of Jamila's muffled hooves. But instead, staccato footsteps rang up the path she'd taken. *They found me!*

Up ahead she spotted a battered shop, empty except for a few boxes and remnants of ribbons and buttons littering the ground. Before she could dive in, a voice hissed behind her.

"Nadia, where are you?"

Her steps faltered at the familiar voice, and she turned around. A round face, pale with fear, appeared in the murky light.

"Basel!" Nadia cried with relief, amazed at how he'd slipped past the rebels and found her.

He smiled, though his lips were strained. "I couldn't leave you. Tarek was taking care of Ammo, so I came."

Nadia pulled him in for a hug.

"We have to go," he wheezed, voice muffled in her coat. "There are rebels crawling through the *souq*."

"But now we're both lost," she said.

"Ammo Mazen told me to meet up at the northeast gate," he said. "Bab al-Hadid gate."

They fled, racing through the crisscrossed alleys of the *souq*, the floor littered with fragments of cord, rope, and torn fabric. Near the exit, an arched stone gate, they slowed, a familiar noise resonating from outside. . . . *Rain.*

"Look," whispered Basel, pointing past a line of sooty sheets.

A grove of palm trees grew along the edge of a pedestrian walkway that ran along the base of a massive hilltop. According to tradition, this was where Prophet Abraham once herded his sheep. Nearly two hundred feet high, its pale limestone slope pockmarked with mortar and bomb blasts, the hill carried the citadel as its crown, the multistoried facade embedded with windows edged with white-and-black stone. Now a red, white, and black Syrian flag flew from the ramparts, evidence of government occupation. Ammo Mazen's words rang in her head. *The citadel is under Syrian army control . . . snipers posted along the top.*

Basel tugged on her arm, pointing left, toward the

Carlton Citadel Hotel. She glimpsed a group of men in fatigues sheltering behind a line of burned-out cars. Heavy machine guns and rocket launchers lay stacked beside them.

"Are they rebels?" whispered Nadia.

Basel shrugged. "Not sure, but whoever they are, they're about to have a fight with someone."

Nadia tensed. They needed to get out of there before they were caught in the middle of a battle. Fingering the silver pin, she racked her brain, staring at the open expanse of the walkway. She inched forward to get a better view in the gray light. *If it's hard for me to see, they probably can't see much either.* With a grim smile she unhooked a sooty sheet hanging from a length of rope.

Chapter Twenty-Eight

October 11, 2013 6:07 p.m.

Hunched beneath the dirty, tattered sheet, Nadia and Basel hid themselves from potential onlookers and exited the handicraft market into the fading light of dusk. They wove through the palm trees and paused behind a tree trunk.

"Look for snipers," she whispered, as she focused on the entrance to the citadel. It stood two hundred feet to their right. Wide steps led up to the guard tower that provided access to the bridge. Built of sandstone blocks, the bridge spanned the moat, supported by eight soaring arches. A memory flickered in her mind, of holding her father's hand and skipping up those same steps, eager to glimpse the stunning views of the city. Beyond the bridge rose the main gates into the citadel, the door damaged by shells when rebels launched a failed assault. And beyond the gates lay the heart of the fortress, where she'd spent hours wandering the maze of archaeological sites that had always reminded her of a cake, the different layers revealing slices of history: Greek foundations, Roman artifacts, Byzantine ruins, and a series of barracks, palaces, bathhouses, and mosques constructed by Salaheddine's son, Mamluk Arabs, and the Ottomans.

From under the sheet, Basel eyed the slits in the fortress wall where archers had once launched arrows at attackers below. "I don't see any snipers up there," he whispered.

"Good," Nadia muttered, hoping they were inside because of the rain. She and Basel would have to circle the base of the hill until they could melt into a side street going north toward the gate. Streets radiated outward from the hill like spokes on a wheel.

"I can't see anything happening back at the hotel either," said Basel.

Nadia breathed a sigh of relief. Just maybe, the downpour would prove to be their savior. "Let's go," she whispered.

Together, they shuffled across the pedestrian walkway toward the low boundary wall that ran along the base of the hill. But as they approached, Nadia's relief came to an abrupt end. The rat-a-tat of machine-gun fire sounded up ahead, and muffled shouts rang out from the esplanade. "The men from the *souq*," she whispered. "They've doubled back and are heading toward us."

"What?" croaked Basel in disbelief.

A ragged breath caught in Nadia's throat as she eyed the expanse of the walkway to their right, slick with rain. *Nowhere to hide . . .*

Before she could think what to do next, Basel pulled her down beside the base of the boundary wall and secured the sheet around them. "I hope we look like a big old rock," he muttered.

What do we do now? Nadia stared through a tear in the sheet, desperately looking for an escape. Her gaze fell on the bridge that linked the guard tower to the main gates of the citadel, a route she'd taken many times on past visits. "This way, to the citadel," she hissed, grabbing Basel's hand, and half running, half crawling toward the citadel steps about a hundred feet away.

"We can't go in there," hissed Basel, resisting. "We'll be dead for sure!"

"We're not going all the way up," said Nadia. "Just to the guard tower till things calm down."

"I don't know about this . . . ," muttered Basel, but followed.

Through the hole in the sheet, Nadia kept an eye on the guard tower as they scurried along the boundary wall as fast as they could. *Eighty more feet . . . thirty . . . ten more.* She glanced beyond the tower toward the bridge. "Oh no," she gasped. Grabbing Basel's hand, she pulled him down to the base of the wall.

"Ouch," grumbled Basel, rubbing his elbow. "What did you do that for?"

"Sorry," said Nadia. "The doors to the citadel are open. Soldiers are coming down the bridge."

"What do we do now?"

Anger and fear flared through her. *Yes, what do we do now?* Feeling hopeless, she punched the wall with a clenched fist, about to admit defeat. The concrete sent a shock of pain rattling against her knuckles. *The wall . . .*

Booted feet stomped along the walkway, weapons rattling, breaths heavy, the air crackling with tension. Nadia and Basel sat six inches away, scrunched over, on the other side of the boundary wall. With seconds to spare, they'd climbed over the waist-high concrete barrier that separated the walkway from the lip of the moat, before the rebels could spot them. Meanwhile, the Syrian soldiers exiting the main gates of the citadel had made their way across the bridge to the guard tower and had barricaded themselves inside.

"Come on," said Nadia, heart pounding as she shoved the sheet into her backpack. The rain had picked up, and it soaked them to the bone as they slithered down the steep embankment slick with mud. The moat stretched along the bottom, passing under the stone arches supporting the bridge. Water pooled in the usually dry ditch, swirling past fragments of wall that had tumbled down from the hill. Nadia grabbed Basel's hand and sloshed through the icy puddles, hurrying toward the protection of the arches, about seventy feet away.

"I don't like this," whispered Basel, his usually confident voice wavering. "I don't know how to swim."

"It's okay," panted Nadia, dragging him on. "It isn't very deep—I'll help you."

Basel's grip tightened, and without warning he

halted. Irritated, Nadia glanced back and caught the look of horror on his face. Something floated by, then caught on a jagged outcropping of rock: torn jeans . . . a bloodied shirt. She glimpsed a young face, bloated and pale. Eyes wide, she couldn't help but think that the dead boy looked like her brother. *Jad, that could be Jad,* she thought, *or Malik, or my dad. . . .* Her mind froze.

"Nadia," Basel cried, "we have to go. . . ."

But Nadia stood rooted to the spot, paralyzed. Basel pushed her forward, and icy currents lapped against her legs. She winced as rough stone grazed her cheek when she stumbled under the safety of the bridge. Basel stared at her, fear pooling in his eyes. "Are you okay?" he whispered apprehensively. "Please be okay. . . ."

Nadia slumped against the wall, eyes squeezed shut. *I'm not okay,* she thought, her body shivering uncontrollably. *I can't do this anymore. I can't save Basel—I nearly got him killed. I can't save anyone . . . not even myself.* Basel's skinny arms circled her waist, and his cold face pressed against her neck. Startled, she opened her eyes to see the little boy hugging her as if his life depended on it.

A terrible boom echoed above. Her head jerked up,

and she expected an explosion or a jet roaring past. But when a blinding streak of lightning illuminated the citadel so that it glowed like a golden beacon against the darkening sky, she realized it was thunder. *"Ya Haddad . . . ,"* she muttered, as Basel tightened his arms.

"*Ya* what?" he mumbled against her skin.

A memory tugged at her mind . . . a cool spring day, when she was about ten. An apple-cheeked history student from the university was giving Nadia's family a tour. Vivacious and full of stories about the secret tunnels and dungeons that ran beneath the citadel, she'd led the family to the heart of the complex, to its oldest site. A basalt sphinx and lion guarded the entrance to an ancient temple that housed a stone carving: a powerful bearded figure wearing a bull-horned headdress and carrying a thunderbolt.

"*Ya* what?" repeated Basel.

Nadia took a deep breath, her pulse calmer. "Remember the Ebla tablet we saw at Professor Laila's hideout?" At his nod, she continued, "Haddad was the storm god from that time. He was known as the protector of life and growing things. His temple is in the heart of the citadel."

"Maybe he's protecting us," said Basel, as another strike of lightning brightened the skies.

With a pained grin, Nadia hugged Basel back, wanting to keep him safe as she would her little brother. *Protecting us. Yes,* she thought with returning determination. "Come," she said, "we need to go."

"Do you think Ammo Mazen and Tarek have reached the gate and are waiting for us?" asked Basel.

"They might have," answered Nadia, pulling out the compass.

"Which way do we go?" asked Basel, his teeth chattering.

"We follow the curve of the moat," she said. "Once we're on the other side of the citadel, we'll climb out and make our way to the gate."

"Bab al-Hadid gate," said Basel. "Sounds like the god Haddad."

"Right," said Nadia, with what she hoped was an encouraging smile. She eyed the moat and was about to emerge from under the arch when shouts rang out above them. She shrank back into the shadows. Basel stood peering down at the water swirling around their ankles. Nadia looked up at the boundary wall where they'd climbed over. It was quiet. The men had disappeared, at least for the moment. She knew the lull wouldn't last. . . . A clash was coming.

Half an hour later, they ducked behind a car parked at a roundabout. "There it is," whispered Nadia. Bab al-Hadid. The iron gate. They looked through the arched doorway that led into a stone tower, hoping for a glimpse of Ammo Mazen or Tarek. But there was no movement.

"Maybe they're inside the tower," whispered Basel.

"They should have been here a long time ago," muttered Nadia, looking for the cart or Jamila.

"Maybe they got stuck somewhere along the way," said Basel matter-of-factly.

She nodded, trying to appear positive, but she couldn't stop herself from running through the possibilities: *shot by snipers, bombed, caught by rebels . . .*

"We'll just wait," said Basel, pointing to a spot behind an empty newspaper kiosk, which they barricaded with empty crates and cardboard.

Nadia slumped beside him and looked down at her hands, surprised to see that her mittens had disappeared, leaving chipped and torn nails. She stared at the flecks of nail polish and froze, expecting a familiar sense of panic to flood her chest. But it didn't come. *I don't really care,* she thought. She looked out between a gap in the cardboard and stared at the moon. She wondered where her family was and whether they were gazing at the same moon, safe on the Turkish border. Releasing a hot gush of air from her lungs, she continued staring at the silver orb, dancing between the clouds, a flickering beacon.

Chapter Twenty-Nine

January 13, 2013

Nadia hadn't seen Ms. Darwish in over six months. Not since that last day at school, the day before the school permanently shut its doors after months of dwindling enrollment and growing violence on the streets. But there she was, in the middle of the night, her sharp features framed by a plum scarf, her figure leaner. She enveloped Nadia in a warm hug and introduced her brother, Safwan, a police captain. Although Nadia was surprised to see her, her parents weren't. The four of them disappeared into the living room with stern instructions that they were not to be disturbed.

Like many across Syria, Ms. Darwish's Sunni family had been fractured by differing loyalties. One faction believed in ending years of tyranny by supporting the rebels. The other side, however, saw Assad, no matter how terrible he was, as the only force that could hold Syria together, allowing them to live in relative peace and comfort. They'd seen how other countries in the region, like Iraq, had turned into a living hell after their dictators, Saddam Hussein in Iraq's case, had been toppled. They didn't want Syria to suffer that same fate. Ms. Darwish's father supported the regime, and he'd decided to move his wife and their children, along with spouses and grandchildren, to Damascus. But before she left, Ms. Darwish fulfilled a request Nadia's mother had made to her in a desperate phone call the day before. And as Nadia later learned, Safwan had unearthed the information they needed, using his extensive contacts with the *mukhabarat*.

The evening after Ms. Darwish's visit, Khala Shakira sat, too shocked to even weep. But Razan, huddled beside her mother, was doubled over with sobs. The entire family was crammed into her and Nadia's grandparents' living room, and even the little kids were there, silent as mice.

"Are you sure it's him?" asked Jiddo, eyes hopeful as he stared at Ammo Ramzi, standing with Khala Lina.

Nadia's father shook his head, face drained of color. "It was just like Safwan told us last night; the *mukhabarat* picked Zayn up for interrogation. After we bribed the right people, we found him."

"Are you sure?" repeated Jiddo.

"Yes, Father, it's Zayn," said Ammo Hadi. "We're certain."

"What happened?" whispered Nana, her usually calm demeanor frayed.

"He was found near the soccer stadium, in a ditch," said Nadia's father.

"Was it the *mukhabarat*?" asked Jiddo, his face aging before their eyes, his body trembling.

"That's what we've heard," said Ammo Hadi.

"He shouldn't have gone back to the office," said Nana, face drained of color.

"They came twice to interview him, and when he didn't provide answers they liked, they took him," whispered Nadia's father.

Silence descended on the room. Tears streamed down Nadia's face as the phrase *took him* repeated in her head like a DVD caught on repeat. She knew what that meant. To be taken by the *mukhabarat* meant a visit to the government's prisons to be interrogated, tortured . . . killed. An image of her uncle flashed before her, of a man filled with laughter, always telling terrible jokes and bringing home chocolate for the kids. The day they found him, hands and feet bound, a single bullet in his head, was the day Jiddo had the stroke that took his life. It was the day her grandmother's hair turned white and Khala Shakira stopped talking.

Later that week, Nadia's father, uncles, and male cousins stood before Nana. "You must give us permission, Mother," Nadia's father pleaded, standing tall in his olive-green woolen coat. "You know we cannot go without your consent."

But Nana stayed silent, face haggard. She was dressed in widow's garb. "How can you ask this of me?" she finally asked, eyes bright with unshed tears. "Zayn and your father are gone. Now you're asking to risk your lives?"

"Mother," said Ammo Hadi. "We're not safe. Our city and country are no longer safe."

"Hadi is right," echoed Ammo Ramzi. "We must do something."

Nadia stood in the shadows, shivering. What her

uncle said was true. Within days of Ammo Zayn's body being found, an old family friend had come by, slipping through the back door. He'd stayed only a few minutes, just long enough to share what he'd learned. Authorities believed Ammo Zayn had been supplying phosphate to rebels to build bombs. Now the family's name was on a list of potential enemies.

"We can no longer hide our heads in the sand like ostriches," continued Ammo Hadi. "Assad is out to erase us from the earth. We have to do something to save our family, our country."

With tears streaming down her cheeks, Nana gave them permission to go. So on a chilly January night the men melted away into the darkness to join the rebels. Soon the family received texts with smiling pictures of the men, holding machine guns, giving thumbs-up signs. Over the next few months, Nadia and her aunts and cousins sat huddled beside the television and radio and on the Internet, collecting news. They heard that the Kurds in the north, most notably the Kurdish Saladin Brigade, were working with other opposition forces, like her father's, to create a multireligious and multiethnic coalition. But then rumors began to bubble of rebel groups using civilian homes for shelter, looting supplies, and switching loyalties from one group to another. Things worsened when foreign fighters began arriving from around the world. Many were experienced and came from the ongoing insurgencies in neighboring Iraq; others were novices, emboldened by religious extremism, come to Syria to play at war.

"We are being squeezed," wrote Nadia's father in a text late one night. "On one side by Assad's forces, on the other by warring rebel groups and foreign fighters. We are losing hope. . . . The country is falling apart before our eyes . . ."

Chapter Thirty

October 11, 2013 9:07 p.m.

Nadia stared at her watch. *Where can they be?* she thought for the thousandth time, worry burning through her like acid. They'd been waiting for over an hour and the only thing that had crossed their path had been a stray dog and a few mice. Not that Basel had noticed; he'd been fast asleep. Nadia stared across the street at a mural of a Free Syrian Army fighter, bleeding in the faint light from the window above. Beneath it the caption read *People, forgive us if we make mistakes. We are dying for you.* Over it someone had spray-painted *Liar*.

Restless, she rose, rubbing away the ache in her leg, anxious to check the gate again. This time she decided to pass through to the other side, and made her way past a line of shuttered blacksmith shops. A cool breeze whistled by, carrying with it a familiar fragrance—the earthy scent of laurel oil, coupled with olive oil and lye. Nadia shone her flashlight into a small abandoned workshop and found fragments of green bars scattered on the ground: Nana's favorite soap, manufactured in Aleppo for over a thousand years. As she circled back to the kiosk, Nadia nearly missed the fluttering cloth tied to a pole beside the tower entrance, a red-and-white-checked scarf. Her heart leapt into her throat. Tarek's *keffiyeh*. Untying it with shaking fingers, she felt a piece of paper knotted inside.

"Are you sure this is it?" asked Basel, examining the nails that studded the heavy wooden door that stood before them. Nadia double-checked the directions drawn on the page and nodded. With the butt of his gun, he rapped against the wood.

Within a minute the door opened a crack, then flew open, revealing a disheveled Tarek. "Thank *Allah* you found us," he said, voice tight with emotion, as Basel threw himself at him for a hug. He and Nadia grinned at each other like idiots. "Another ten minutes and I was going to go looking for you."

"You left great instructions," said Nadia, handing

him back his scarf. "How did you find this place?"

"Ammo Mazen knew the owner and said it would be safe," explained Tarek, locking the doors once they'd slipped through.

"Wow," said Basel, eyes wide as he saw what lay beyond.

Wow, indeed, thought Nadia, staring at a lush garden, illuminated by the moon. A beautiful tiled courtyard, its walls decorated with intricate geometric designs, sat in the center. A marble fountain edged with sweet basil and white roses gurgled in the middle. Beyond it rose a two-story house that reminded her of the one in Jdeideh, where they'd found the figs, but this was far grander.

"Jamila," cried Nadia, spotting the donkey happily chomping on leaves. She ran over to circle her neck with her arms. "Where's Ammo Mazen? Is he okay?"

"He's inside," said Tarek, pointing to the doors of the reception hall, standing opposite the *iwan*, the outside sitting area.

Nadia hurried through the doors to find a cheery fire in the fireplace, its warmth spreading over a ball of orange fur curled up against an old man lying on a cushioned divan with his eyes closed. Worry ate at her as she examined his pale face. "Ammo," she whispered, kneeling down next to him. "Are you okay?"

The old man's eyes fluttered open. "Oh my goodness." He stared down at her with relief. "I'm fine, my dear, how are you? Whatever took you so long?"

For the next half hour, they exchanged stories of what had happened after they'd been separated. Mishmish, who'd disappeared after snuggling with Nadia, returned, a dead mouse dangling from his mouth.

Basel took one look at the plump mouse and said wistfully, "I'm hungry. Do you think there's any food?"

Only he could look at a dead rodent and think of food, thought Nadia, exchanging a smile with Tarek. Leaving Ammo Mazen to rest, they used Nadia's flashlight to forage through the house, passing through a hallway into another sitting room, its ceiling inlaid with colored marble, its walls supporting built-in shelves crammed with statues and carvings. Through another hall, they finally stumbled into the kitchen.

"Nothing . . . there's nothing," grumbled Basel, poking his head into an empty cupboard as Tarek yanked open drawers crammed with utensils.

Nadia peered behind the stove, hoping to find a

bouillon cube, a crust of dried bread, or fallen grains of rice, but sighed in disappointment. A rank, moldy smell spilled from the fridge, which was empty except for a half bottle of milk, curdled and green. Frustrated, she slammed it shut, thinking of the unlimited number of free cartons of dried milk she'd gotten from the dairy company after her advertisement ran. She peered behind the fridge, just in case. *Nothing . . .*

"It looks like they took it all with them," said Tarek, disappointed, as he grabbed a stack of candles he'd found in the back of a cupboard.

"Maybe I can find a pigeon or something," said Basel.

"In the morning," said Tarek, patting him on the shoulder. "For now, we should just get some rest."

"We'll go look for blankets," said Nadia as they each took a lit candle from Tarek. "Why don't you keep an eye on Ammo?"

Trying to ignore the ache gnawing at her insides, Nadia led Basel back to the front door, where a set of stairs led to the second floor. The final step opened out onto an airy sitting room. She headed toward the first door. A double bed sat against the wall, covered with a frilly pink duvet, a jumble of toys littering the floor. A desk sat below the shuttered window, piled with art supplies.

Basel hurried over to examine a pad of fine white paper and an expensive set of colored pencils. "This is so nice," he whispered.

Nadia spotted a CD player and small set of speakers sitting on the bookshelf. It was similar to a set Jad had often let her use. She flipped it on eagerly. *It works,* she thought happily. *The batteries are charged.* She'd have to find some CDs. She inched along a wide bookshelf, holding her candle. *Books* . . . She thought fondly of the hours she'd spent reading to Basel, appreciating Scheherazade's ability to take them on a journey through words. A familiar title caught her eye, one her brother and cousins had fought over when they first got it. They'd tried to get her to read it too, but the idea of plodding through such a thick book about a boy wizard hadn't interested her much. She pulled it out and flipped through the pages, a paragraph catching her eye.

> *He had never seen so many things he liked to eat on one table: roast beef, roast chicken, pork chops*

and lamb chops, sausages, bacon and steak, boiled potatoes, roast potatoes, fries, Yorkshire pudding, peas, carrots, gravy, ketchup, and, for some strange reason, peppermint humbugs.

Nadia stared at the words, saliva pooling in her mouth. Before she realized what she was doing, she crumpled the page, ready to stuff it in her mouth. She stopped herself in time and smoothed the paper with a shaking hand.

"This is a warm one," said Basel, lugging the duvet, along with the art supplies.

Nadia tucked the book under her arm, grabbed the CD player, and headed to the room across the hall. An unmade bed sat along a wall lined with posters of sports cars. Basel tiptoed past clothes strewn across the floor to check out a huge stereo sitting next to a broken computer monitor. *Definitely a boy's room,* she thought. *A teenage boy.* She instructed Basel to grab some dry clothes for himself and Tarek, and headed to the other room across the hall. The door swung open but stopped short, thudding against something solid. The flashlight revealed a fancy master bedroom, filled with ornate furniture and heavy silk drapes. About to step inside, she sniffed something . . . *something rotten*. She knew from experience that it wasn't the stink of a dead body, and even though her instincts told her to leave it alone, she inched forward and peered behind the door. It was a canvas bag, left by someone in a hurry. Curiosity got the best of her and she held her nose and yanked open the zipper. Inside lay a plastic bag, dripping with soggy tomatoes and cucumbers, reduced to green slime. Beneath it sat another bag, with maggots crawling over a chunk of meat. She jerked away, kicking the canvas in disgust. But as her foot hit the bag, she heard a distinctive clang.

Nadia awoke with a start, Mishmish curled up beside her head, cold nose in her ear. She lay there, wondering if it had all been a dream. *But it wasn't,* she thought. They'd feasted on canned grape leaves stuffed with rice and pine nuts, sweet corn, corned beef, stewed okra, and sardines. And cookies, though a bit stale, and hot tea liberally sweetened with honey. As they'd sat in front of the fire in dry clothes, Nadia had taught the boys card games she'd played with her cousins, and for the first time in months, she'd been rolling on the floor, laughing at Basel's antics and Tarek's dry jokes. Even Ammo Mazen had perked up and given Basel advice on how to play his hand. But when Nadia helped fix a plate of food for the old man, she'd been struck by how feeble he'd become, eyes dull, thin cheeks sunken. The exertion of the last few days had taken their toll. Deeply troubled, she'd handed him two pills from his bottle, and after swallowing them, he'd lain down.

Now, snuggled beneath a fluffy pink bedspread, she watched the embers from the fire, thinking that despite all that had happened so far, they were still alive. *Insha'Allah*, they'd be in Turkey soon, with her family. She slipped out from beneath her covers. Ammo Mazen and Tarek still slept, but Basel sat hunched over a coffee table, his fingers flying across the crisp white paper, pencils in hand. Creeping up from behind, Nadia peered over his shoulder. She was amazed by what she saw. A pigeon, its feathers glinting, took flight across one page. Beside it was an intricate silver astrolabe, like they'd seen at Professor Laila's secret hideout. But it was the picture he was currently drawing that caught her breath. In black, gray, and red, a little boy stood huddled next to an old woman, a basket of lemons in her hand. A helicopter flew above, spraying bullets over a collapsed apartment building. Bodies lay on the grass, blood seeping into the dirt. Her heart constricted. All this time, he hadn't said a word about what he'd been through, but here it was, in picture form.

Alef Layla, she thought. *I should read him a story . . . to get his mind off things.* She hurried out of the house and greeted Jamila with a gentle scratch under her chin before going to the cart. The air was crisp and clean, the sky a bright shade of blue. As she reached for the tarp, she noticed that the cart looked banged up, damaged from its wild ride through the *souq*. Ammo Mazen's hidden compartment was wide open, the lock broken. Worried that his important possessions had tumbled out, she reached inside. Her fingers encountered cold metal . . . *the gun*. She nudged it aside, reached further inside, and encountered the velvet bag, bulging with gold bars and banknotes. Trapped behind it lay a plastic bag. Relief flowed over her, and something else. *Curiosity.* Before she realized what she was doing, she tugged it forward. In her rush, the flimsy plastic caught on a bent nail, sending the contents flying to the ground:

over a dozen badges and identification cards. Confused, she bent to pick them up.

They all had pictures of Ammo Mazen at various ages. *But the names . . . they're different,* she thought. She picked up an old, faded card. A smiling teenager stared back at her, familiar eyes sparkling with amber flecks. The name on the card was Ahmed Mazen Makhlouf. *Ahmed. That's what Sulaiman called him.* Her eyes fell on the *qayd*, his father or grandfather's village or neighborhood of origin. *Qardaha. Ya Allah,* she thought, eyes fixed in disbelief. It was the ancestral village of the Assad family, where Hafez and his eldest son were buried. *But Ammo Mazen said he was from Aleppo. . . .* Her memory sorted through their conversations over the past few days. *He said he was from a mountain village . . . but there are no mountains in Aleppo. He had been lying.* With shaking fingers, she lifted up an official-looking badge with a middle-aged Ahmed Mazen Makhlouf, face stern, hair dark and wavy. Over a white collared shirt, he wore a black leather jacket. His job, listed on the badge, was that of a commander of the *mukhabarat*.

Chapter Thirty-One

October 12, 2013 4:21 p.m.

It was late afternoon by the time they reluctantly left the idyllic courtyard house that had given them protection and sustenance. Tarek had stumbled onto a map of the country in an office in the back of the house. They'd pored over it, Ammo Mazen pointing out the best route with a shaky hand while Nadia traced it with a red pencil. Rested and fed, with no more errands to distract them, they efficiently trudged north through the last bit of the city, avoiding the main roads and circumventing rebel checkpoints. Thankfully, there weren't many. What would have taken them less than half an hour by car was taking them four hours on foot.

At least it isn't raining, thought Nadia with a shiver, glancing up at the darkening sky. She tightened her coat against the bitter wind, her thoughts deeply troubled as she glanced back at Tarek, who followed behind the cart. *I should have told him what I found.*

After quickly returning the identification cards to the secret compartment and sealing it as best she could, she'd gone back to the sitting room with *Alef Layla* tucked under her arm. She felt dizzy with the agony of betrayal, anger, and fear swirling inside her. She'd wanted to jerk Tarek awake and tell him what she'd learned, then confront Ammo Mazen. Instead, she'd paused at the door, watching them sleep in the only precious stretch of peace they'd had in days. She had added wood to the fire and read the tale of Nur al-Din and Miriam the Sash-Maker to Basel, hoping to talk to Tarek as soon as he woke up.

But Ammo Mazen had woken first, shivering, lungs struggling to pull in raspy breaths. Alarmed, Nadia piled on blankets and gave him two pills, just as Tarek hurried over. He'd been at the old man's side since then, whispering desperate prayers for health, while Basel gave him sips of hot tea. Nadia's anger deflated like a punctured balloon, though a needle of betrayal remained. From the moment she'd met the old man, he'd surprised her at every turn. He could have left her at the pharmacy or the dental office, but he'd promised to help her and then the boys too. Perhaps they did provide some kind of cover from pursuers, but he'd kept his word, as he had with so many others: Alaa, Professor Laila, the bishop, and even her beloved Haleb, by saving its historical artifacts with his secretive ways. Over the past few days, she'd been softened by his kindness, and in turn had grown to love him in an odd way. But her affection for him warred with the truth that he had lied about who he was.

Does it matter? whispered a voice at the edge of her mind. Yes, he was a *mukhabarat* commander, but he definitely didn't act like one now. Frustrated, she kicked a rock from the road, savoring the pain as it connected with her toe. It also jolted her back to reality: They'd reached the northern edge of the city.

"Stop," whispered Nadia, bringing Jamila to a halt beside a silent office building that rose along a wide, two-lane road. On the other side they could see hulking, shadowy structures; it was the sprawling industrial complex, home to factories, machine shops, and warehouses. Her grandfather had once owned a phosphate processing plant here; they'd sold it many years back to invest in a larger factory. The main highway north lay just beyond the plant, slightly to the west.

"It's really quiet," said Basel in a hushed voice.

Nadia nodded, taking a deep breath. She glanced back at Tarek.

"Ammo is asleep," he whispered.

"We need to keep moving," said Nadia, gently nudging Jamila across the road. As they made their way through the deserted jungle of factories, many stripped of machinery and equipment, she relaxed, and dug around in her backpack to pull out a CD she'd found in the boy's room. She slipped it into the CD player, hoping to push away the warring emotions in her head. She yelped in pain as a harsh screeching pummeled her eardrums, forcing her to yank out the earbuds. "Ow," she grumbled, turning it off. The stupid thing was supposed to be ballads by Amr Diab; instead it was some awful techno, give-yourself-a-headache-type stuff. Not wanting to waste the batteries, she slipped it back into her pack, next to the speakers and other odds and ends she'd scavenged from the house thinking they might be needed at the refugee camp.

Nadia's thoughts turned north to Turkey, imagining what it would be like. Life would not be easy there, she knew. After her family had made the decision to go, she'd sought out pictures and news clips of the refugee camps, and the images had scared her: rows and rows of overcrowded tents, little or no access to jobs for adults or schools for kids, inhabitants jostling for food, water, and medicine. But it was better than here, and she'd be with her family, which was the most important thing. What came after was in *Allah*'s hands. She sighed, glancing at Mishmish, who sat at his favorite spot near Jamila's tail. He was licking himself, trying to get rid of the dust and grime on his matted fur. As she grinned at his fastidiousness, he paused, ears cocked, nose twitching.

"There's a fire burning somewhere," said Basel, sniffing as he stared at the sky, studded with a shimmer of stars, a backdrop for a nearly full moon.

The acrid smell of burning rubber grew stronger as they plodded northwest along the dark and narrow roads that wound through the complex. Nadia led them past a series of desolate processing plants, factories, and abandoned warehouses. Along the way they saw a few small restaurants that had once served the thousands of workers who'd labored here. Nadia was tempted to search a small café for supplies; a cup of hot sweet tea was so very tempting. *But there's no time,* she thought with a sigh. She eyed a warehouse on the other side of the road and caught a familiar scent bobbing in the wind. *Phosphate,* she thought, the metallic tinge tickling her nose.

"Something is not right," muttered Basel, tugging at her coat sleeve and pointing to a plume of smoke rising from the other side of a brand-new building on the left, its construction halted because of the war.

Nadia nodded, cautiously pulling in Jamila, who balked at being slowed. The smell of smoke was stronger as they passed bulldozers stalled on the side of the road and an idle crane leaning against the building's rooftop. Nadia was about to call out to Tarek that they should stop, but Jamila got it into her head to pick up her pace. She trotted around a bulldozer and along the length of the building, waking Ammo Mazen. As the kids ran to keep up, Ammo Mazen sat up, gripping the sides of the cart. It wasn't until they stumbled onto a sprawling parking lot that Jamila slowed. They glimpsed flames, partially obscured by a line of broken-down cars.

"Children, turn back," whispered Ammo Mazen. "This doesn't look safe." Nadia pulled on Jamila's reins, but it was too late.

Half a dozen shadowy figures stood around the fire, which blazed in a metal drum. "Stop!" shouted an imposing young man, as he and the others—teenagers, really—circled around them like a pack of wolves. Scruffy, bloodied, wearing mismatched military fatigues, they carried an odd assortment of guns and knives. Nadia and the boys huddled around the cart, Mishmish hissing. Before she knew what she was doing, Nadia unhooked his leash, and a blur of orange disappeared into the darkness.

The one who'd told them to stop stepped forward. "What have we here?" he drawled with a wolfish grin.

"We are merely passing through," said Ammo Mazen, holding up his hands.

"I'll be the one to determine that," said the leader. "Got any money? Food?"

"I'm afraid we don't have any money, but you are welcome to our food," said Ammo Mazen, voice calm, wincing as he tried to move. Tarek and Basel reached out to help. He'd barely descended from the cart when the leader yanked off the tarp and began to paw through the tools and utensils. Nadia eyed the secret compartment. She glanced up and spotted a smooth-cheeked boy, no older than seventeen, standing across from them. Catching Nadia's gaze, he lowered his gaze, ashamed. But he did nothing to stop the others from rifling through Ammo Mazen's things.

The leader took the cans of food they'd saved and tossed it to his friends. "This will barely feed three of us," he growled, eyeing Jamila. "We'll eat this nag. It'll be tasty, grilled."

Shaking, fists clenched, Tarek stepped forward. "You *can't* eat her," he croaked.

"Of course we can," said the leader.

"It's . . . it's *haram*, religiously not allowed, to eat a donkey," Tarek tried to reason. "Horses and mules are okay as food, but *not* a donkey."

"Haram?" snickered the leader. "Who are you to give me a religious lecture?"

"You will be judged for your misdeeds," blurted Tarek. "And punished!"

Shut up . . . , thought Nadia, tugging on Tarek's shirt.

"Punished?" growled the leader. "Are you going to punish *me*, little man?"

Blood drained from Tarek's face, leaving it ghostly white.

Ammo Mazen stood shivering, his face pale, eyes distressed. "Young man, I understand your desperation, but this donkey—" He stopped short as the leader lunged forward and slammed the butt of his rifle into his forehead.

A scream rose up from Nadia's throat as she stared at the old man, knocked unconscious.

"Shut up!" yelled the leader, grabbing Jamila's reins. "Get lost."

Nadia stared bleakly at the poor animal as they pulled her toward the fire, beating her with a stick when she resisted.

"We have to go," urged Basel, trembling as he eyed the retreating figures.

"Yes," croaked Nadia. "Before they think to come back for us."

Together, they lifted Ammo Mazen's frail body

and hurried back the way they'd come. Nadia held the old man's head, amazed how light he was. When they turned the corner she caught a final glimpse of Jamila as the men tied her to a light pole at the edge of the lot before passing out the cans. *At least they're eating that first,* she thought.

"This way," said Tarek, leading them to the warehouse on the other side of the road. Past the rusted metal door, they found themselves in a dilapidated space littered with burlap bags. They gently placed the old man on the ground so he could lean against a lumpy bag.

"What kind of animals attack an old man?" growled Nadia as she and Tarek knelt to inspect Ammo's forehead.

"That is an insult to animals," muttered Tarek, gently probing the bruise. "Animals only attack if they're looking for food or scared."

"Thankfully, his skull is fine," said Nadia with relief.

"What are we going to do?" whispered Basel, voice full of tears.

Nadia closed her eyes, panic looming as she gripped her bright silver pin. But instead of wanting to hide in a dark corner like she usually did, she felt a strange sense of calm settle over her. What had Ms. Darwish said? *Unlimited possibilities,* that's what the pin represented. Her eyes flickered open and she stared at each boy in turn. "We have to get Jamila back," she said. "Without her and the cart, there's no way we're getting Ammo Mazen to Turkey."

"How are we going to do that?" asked Tarek, face tight with exhaustion and worry.

"Yeah, how?" wailed Basel, pacing.

"Pray," said Tarek, wringing his hands. "We all need to pray. . . ."

Nadia stood clutching the silver brooch, a gift that represented the great expectations that Ms. Darwish had had for her. *Misplaced expectations,* she thought bitterly.

"We also need guns," muttered Basel, arms empty. His grandfather's rifle was back on the cart. "Or an army or something . . ."

Something. The word caught in Nadia's mind. *What would Scheherazade do? She would come up with a clever story to distract the king. . . .* "A story, we need a story," she whispered.

The boys looked at her like she'd lost her mind.

"A story?" grumbled Basel. "That's worse than just sitting around and praying!"

"No, no, we need to come up with a diversion, a kind of story to distract those jerks so we can take Jamila and the cart back." Nadia's shoulder's straightened. She took a deep breath and glanced at Ammo Mazen, then to the bag he was leaning on. *Phosphate . . . it's phosphate,* she thought, remembering her brother's crazy experiments. "I have an idea," she gasped, "but I need your help."

Chapter Thirty-Two

October 13, 2013 12:11 a.m.

Nearly two hours later, everything was ready. At least, Nadia hoped and prayed it was. Basel had sneakily surveyed the parking lot half an hour before; the men had been cursing and fighting, trying to find a can opener. For now, Jamila was safe. But they had to act before the sun rose; their plan depended on the cover of darkness.

"You feeling okay about your part?" she asked Basel.

"Uh-huh," he replied, patting the backpack slung over his shoulder.

"And you?" she asked Tarek.

"As ready as I'm going to be," he said, nervously juggling the CD player and speakers.

Nadia nodded, hefting the dummy they'd constructed using burlap sacks from the warehouse. They exited the warehouse and headed into the darkness.

Thirteen minutes later, Nadia sat on the roof of the new building, overlooking the parking lot, the men, Jamila, and the cart. In another seventeen minutes their plan would go into action. For those brief minutes, she sat still, staring south, back toward her beloved Haleb, Aleppo, home. . . . Without power, the city was dark except for a few pinpricks of light, indicating the lucky neighborhoods with generators. What had taken five thousand years to build had taken less than two to ravage. What centuries of sieges, roving armies, mad kings, and natural disasters hadn't been able to destroy had been demolished by its own people.

She wiped away a hot tear that ran down her cheek, and she turned back to the lot. *There's work to do.* She adjusted the sheet over the dummy one last time. It looked nothing like the plain, dirty stretch of cotton she'd picked up at the *souq* to use as a cover. Under Basel's magical fingers, it was a masterpiece: a frightful figure with blazing eyes, jagged teeth, and claws, drawn with pieces of charcoal. She double-checked the ropes that they'd used to rig it to the crane that leaned against the top of the building, and she peeked over the edge to see that the teens were still bickering, having finished off the cans of food. Thankfully, Jamila stood quietly, tied at the edge of the lot.

Somewhere down there Tarek was setting up the CD player and speakers while Basel was busy with his task, transporting the six aluminum packets, each the size of a Pepsi can, in his backpack. The packets contained a mixture of sugar and phosphate, carefully cooked in an iron skillet they'd found at a tea shop; they'd also scavenged aluminum and other supplies, from the abandoned restaurants. The recipe was simple, one Jad had found on the Internet the day Nadia had helped with their experiment. Once the sugar and phosphate cooked down to a dark bubbling mass, Tarek had poured the goop into aluminum foil packets. Basel then quickly inserted a length of long rope to serve as the fuse before the substance hardened.

Nadia hoped Basel had made it around the perimeter of the lot and placed the packets under the broken-down cars. After he completed his task, he was to get as close to Jamila as he could.

"Come on," whispered Nadia, looking for the telltale sign that he'd succeeded. Only then could she and Tarek put their part of the plan in play. The seconds passed with agonizing slowness, but there, down below, Nadia spotted six flames flicker to life.

Basel had lit the ends of the fuses. Sparks ran along the lengths of rope toward the aluminum packets, which erupted in flames. Adrenaline raced through Nadia as she moved toward the crane, watching plumes of thick white smoke rise from the parking lot. Then Nadia heard the screaming, coupled with harsh, guttural howls: the heavy metal CD, played on slow mode. The sound wasn't as loud as she'd hoped, but it caught the attention of the men below.

Good, she thought, pushing the dummy out over the parking lot and letting the rope swing it back and forth.

"Hey," shouted a confused voice. "What's going on?"

"Get up, you idiots!" the leader bellowed.

Nadia couldn't help but grin as the frightful figure flew through the thick smoke, seemingly screaming like an evil *jinni*. Shouts and coughing filled the parking lot, then the loud crack of a gunshot.

"Don't shoot, you idiot," someone shouted through the howls and screams. "You'll hit one of us."

Time to go, Nadia thought, racing down the stairs. As she exited the empty building toward the warehouse, a truck engine rumbled to life in the vicinity of the parking lot. Before she could step out onto the road, someone pulled her into the shadows.

"It's me," whispered Tarek, just as a truck careened past, packed with cursing, coughing teens. Once the taillights of the truck disappeared, Nadia and Tarek raced toward the dark warehouse.

Light from the flashlight revealed Ammo Mazen where they'd left him. And beside him, curled up, was Mishmish. Before Nadia could grab the cat for a hug, a familiar brown muzzle slipped through the door, followed by the cart and Basel.

"You did it!" cried Nadia, running to give him a tight hug.

"Yeah," he said, voice muffled in her coat. "It was easy. I just cut her loose and we snuck back through the smoke."

"Way to go, kid," Tarek said, thumping him on the back.

Nadia moved to pet Jamila and held out a bit of sugar she'd saved from making the smoke bombs. But before Jamila took it from her hand, the faithful donkey hurried to the old man's side, nuzzling his face, her ears twitching.

"He'll be okay, girl," said Nadia, with more confidence than she felt. "Let's get him on the cart and covered with blankets."

Tarek nodded. "They might come back looking for us."

Jamila gently stepped forward, as if she knew she shouldn't jostle her precious cargo.

"You're a good girl," Nadia whispered into her ear, rubbing her shoulder. "The best companion."

Nadia remembered Ammo Mazen's warning to avoid the main roads as she pulled out the compass. They stayed parallel to the main highway, leaving the industrial complex behind. This route was familiar, as her family had come this way to picnic in the countryside for generations. Those picnics seemed like a lifetime ago.

"No towns or villages," said Tarek, squinting toward a sign for the city of Andan. "We don't know who's controlling them, and we don't want to find out."

"Come on, girl," Nadia whispered in Jamila's ear, as the sun rose along the horizon. "Let's get your master to safety." Ignoring the ache in her leg, she led them along a dusty path that wound its way through fields and olive groves, taking cover when they heard the sound of helicopters or the scream of jets above.

"Anything happening to the north?" asked Nadia.

"There is action over there," said Basel, pointing east. Clouds of black smoke billowed into the sky, and they could see a MiG fighter jet flying high above.

They heard, then felt, the thud of bombs falling, which Nadia quickly calculated was over ten miles away. Once the sky was clear, they moved on, the only living thing in their path a herd of sheep.

After they had walked for what seemed like hours, the terrain turned rocky and they spotted a village sitting on a low hill.

"Wait," said Nadia, stopping behind a line of scraggly bushes. She shielded her eyes and squinted at the small group of buildings.

"It looks deserted," said Tarek, eyeing a well at the village's edge.

Nadia licked her parched lips. They hadn't had time to load up on water.

Basel doodled in the sand with his finger as a tiny head popped up from beneath upturned roots. "Look, it's a rat," he muttered.

"No," said Nadia, staring at the familiar honey-colored fur. "It's a hamster."

"How do you know that?" he asked.

"My cousin Razan told me," explained Nadia, aching at the thought of her bossy cousin. "She was studying to be a veterinarian at the university and was always bringing home weird stuff like bones and pelts. Once she brought a hamster skeleton and told me they're native to Syria but ended up as pets all over the world."

"Do they taste good?" asked Basel, causing her and Tarek to burst out in laughter.

"Come on," said Nadia. "It's abandoned."

It was a small farm village, empty of inhabitants. With a few empty plastic bottles in hand, they filled up on water.

"His breathing is becoming more strained," said Tarek as Basel dribbled a few drops on Ammo Mazen's lips. Nadia pressed her ear against his chest to hear his heart—faint but beating. His breathing had become shallower and he was still unconscious.

"Come on," she said.

They ascended another gentle hill, and Nadia paused as she looked down into the narrow valley, rubbing her leg to try to squeeze out the pain.

"Wow," said Basel, staring down at the ruins of an ancient stone city that spread out below them.

"I've heard of places like this," mused Tarek. "Dead cities. There's supposed to be hundreds of them on the outskirts of Aleppo."

"This one is called Kharab Shams," said Nadia, jaw clenched. "That church, from Byzantium times, is nearly two thousand years old."

Basel examined the gray stone shell of the two-story church, with its sloping triangular roof and curved arches, and whistled. "That's pretty old."

"My family used to come here for picnics," continued Nadia, staring at the series of homes, bathhouses, and temples. "All of us sat there," she added, pointing to a grassy knoll where they'd sat on a blanket, eating sandwiches and playing cards, afterward exploring the ruins.

"What wonderful memories you have," said Tarek, a contemplative look on his face.

Startled, Nadia looked at him. "Yes, I do have those."

Basel scooted over to her and gave her a one-armed hug. Before he could step away, Nadia ruffled his hair and wiped her nose with a sniff.

They had been walking for more than eight hours, with a break to rest in between. Now the sun was high in the sky. They'd skirted the nondescript town of Ibbin, which they'd spotted on the map, and were nearing a highway, which they needed to cross to continue north. Tarek recited a prayer as they approached the dusty black strip of road, where a line of wrecked military vehicles lay abandoned.

"Do you see anything?" asked Nadia, squinting from one end of the road to the other.

"It looks clear," said Basel.

"We just need to get across," said Nadia. About a mile down they could see a grove of trees.

"Let's go, then," said Tarek, gently patting Jamila.

Over the lip of the road they went, crossing the lanes until they'd made it to the other side. Exhausted but feeling hopeful, they found a flat, chalky road that wove alongside a vacant farm. Nadia grabbed a wild stalk of barley and chewed on one end, enjoying the fresh, herby taste.

"I need to go to the bathroom," announced Basel, as they veered toward the privacy of the trees.

They wove through a set of heavy pines, then abruptly stopped. In a clearing stood two army tanks, Jeeps, and over two dozen bedraggled men. A red, white, and black flag flew above them, identifying them as a Syrian army battalion.

Chapter Thirty-Three

October 13, 2013 10:48 a.m.

"Children," called out a surprised voice.

Nadia saw a man in the stained khaki uniform of a high-ranking officer, a line of badges pinned to his chest, push through the men. *We're going to die . . . ,* she thought bleakly as he strode toward them.

"Should we run?" whispered Basel.

"No," hissed Nadia, clutching her father's olive-green cap. "It'll make it worse."

"Children," repeated the mustached officer as he hurried toward them. "What are you doing here?"

Knees shaking, Nadia stepped forward. "We . . . we're lost. And our grandfather is sick. . . . We need a doctor."

The man took off his cap and sighed, a look of strain pulling down his cheeks. He glanced back at his men. They looked exhausted and . . . and something else. *Heartbroken.* The officer moved toward the cart to look at the old man. "You should not be here," he said. "A battle is coming, and there are foreign fighters pushing in from the east."

Nadia nodded, not knowing what to say. She hoped he'd just tell them to get lost.

"There is a village about two hours' walk north of here," he said. "It is called Shams. There is a healer there who may be able to help your grandfather."

Nadia's eyebrows shot up in surprise. "A healer?"

"Yes, up that way," he said, pointing past the trees, beyond the barley fields. "Just follow the dirt road and take a right at the cemetery. If you see the outskirts of the city of Azaz, you've gone too far."

"Thank you," stammered Nadia.

"We can go?" asked Basel incredulously.

"Yes, yes," said the man, running a hand through his thinning hair. "Go quickly. And watch out for the black flags flown by those ruthless foreign bastards. If you see them, hide."

It was late afternoon when they came upon the village of Shams. It wasn't much more than a cluster of small buildings and homes constructed of mud bricks. Nadia pulled Jamila to a halt at the edge of an overgrown field so they could investigate. It was similar to all the other farming villages they'd passed, idle and rundown. Empty. She would have thought this one was abandoned too, if it hadn't been for the threads of smoke coming from a few of the houses. Slowly, they walked on, noticing curtains rustling in the windows as they passed. When they neared the middle of town, doors cracked open, revealing half a dozen elderly souls with wary eyes.

A stooped woman in a long colorful dress came out of her house at the end of the street. Her white scarf framed a face that was a road map of deep grooves. "What are you children doing here?" she asked, voice raspy.

"*Salaam alaikum*, grandmother," said Nadia. "Our grandfather, he was taking us to Turkey, but he got sick. We were told there is a healer here."

"I am Umm Anous, the healer," said the woman. Slowly she approached the cart, and inspected Ammo Mazen. He had woken once, taken a sip of water, and fallen back into a deep sleep. "Bring him to my house," the woman ordered.

She soon had Ammo Mazen in a low wooden

bed. Jamila brayed and kicked at the door until she too was allowed inside. She stood watch over the old man, nuzzling his head while Mishmish curled up against his side.

"How is he?" asked Tarek.

"Can you give him some medicine?" added Basel.

"From what I can see, this is no simple ailment," said Umm Anous, holding Ammo Mazen's wrist.

"Wait," said Nadia. She ran out to the cart, praying it was still there. She dug through the back of the cart, now a disorganized jumble. Shoving aside his tools and equipment, she found the familiar leather bag. She paused and stared at the secret compartment. Then she pulled it open and removed everything, including the gun, and tucked it into her coat pocket.

As the old woman examined the bottles, Nadia quietly put Ammo Mazen's possessions inside her backpack and pushed it under the bed.

"These are pain relievers and sedatives," said Umm Anous. "Barely a balm for what truly ails him."

"What's wrong with him?" croaked Nadia, remembering all the times she'd seen him take pills over the past few days.

"It looks like he has been ill for a long time," said Umm Anous.

Basel squeezed Nadia's hand. "But will he be okay?" he asked.

"I do not have anything that will cure him," said Umm Anous with a sigh.

"We have to get him to Turkey," said Nadia. "They will have doctors that can help him there."

"You must let him rest while I make him a restorative broth," said the woman, drawing a thick quilt over him. "When he wakes, we can make a plan."

The old woman led them into a field behind the village. A small garden lay hidden behind shrubs and wooden lattices, which served as protection from marauding soldiers. While Umm Anous and the boys dug through the rich soil, the color of henna, for potatoes and beets, Nadia stood still, her mind on Ammo Mazen, who'd woken up long enough to swallow the broth of restorative herbs. He'd asked where they were and, upon learning that they were safe, dropped back to sleep. Elated that he was getting better, she took in a deep, calming breath, catching a familiar scent. *Petrichor*, her father had called it, she remembered from their conversation on the balcony so long ago. It was the scent produced when rain reacted with the earth. The word had Greek roots—*petra*, "stone," and *ichor*, "blood."

"Before the drought, you could see lush fields of wheat and barley for miles in every direction," said the old woman, lost in the memory.

"My father said the drought is caused by climate change," said Nadia.

"I do not know about such fancy words," said the woman, smiling. "All I know is that nearly seven years ago, it stopped raining. And once the water disappeared, my son and other young people went to the city to find jobs."

"Where is he?" asked Basel, chewing on a sprig of tender mint.

"He was killed," said Umm Anous, her lips pressed in a thin line.

"Oh," coughed Basel, mint stuck in his throat. "I'm sorry."

"Syria is stained with the blood of its people, struggling to find justice," said Umm Anous with a sigh. "May *Allah* grant his mercy so that we find peace soon."

Chapter Thirty-Four

October 13, 2013 9:49 p.m.

"Water . . . ," whispered a faint voice.

Nadia dropped the wooden spoon in the pot of lentil stew on the stove and ran over to the bed with a glass of water. Tarek propped up the old man's head as she pressed the cup to his dry lips.

After a long sip, he said, "My pills . . . please, give me two."

As he swallowed them, Nadia stood at the edge of the bed, the medicine bottle clenched tightly in her hand. *Please, please,* Allah, *please make him better so that we can leave.*

"Thank you," said Ammo Mazen. He leaned back, and his frail body shook with rattling coughs. He covered his mouth with a kerchief, and when he pulled it back, Nadia was horrified to glimpse a dark streak of blood.

"Are you hungry?" asked Tarek.

He shook his head. "Where are we? How long have I been asleep?"

"We're in a village called Shams," explained Tarek. "At a healer's house, the one you met earlier. She stepped out to get some supplies."

"You've been asleep for over twenty-four hours," Basel piped in.

"How did we get here?" asked Ammo Mazen.

While the boys filled him in on how they saved Jamila, Nadia stood at the foot of the bed.

"You did all that?" Ammo gasped in amazement. "What an ingenious idea, Nadia. I'm so proud of you, of all of you."

"We need to leave," interrupted Nadia. "We've wasted enough time."

Ammo Mazen blinked, his face turning sober. "Yes, we must discuss how to continue toward the Turkish border."

"Jamila has been fed and watered, so we just need to get you back onto the cart," said Nadia.

"I'm afraid that's not possible," said Ammo Mazen.

"What do you mean?" said Tarek, frowning.

Ammo Mazen sighed and closed his eyes for a moment, conflicting emotions flickering across his lined face. "Actually, I'm surprised that I've made it this far."

"What do you mean? What's wrong with you?" asked Basel in his usual blunt fashion.

Ammo Mazen opened his eyes. "I have cancer," he said.

"What?" gasped the little boy.

"The doctors gave me three months to live and that was six months ago," he continued. "Every day I've had since has been a blessing."

Cancer? thought Nadia, the ground dropping away from beneath her feet. The sensation of betrayal, which she'd decided to bury, rose up again.

"You didn't tell us," said Tarek, voice tight.

"Son," said Ammo Mazen, "life on this earth is temporary, for everyone."

"You lied," Nadia blurted. "You've lied about everything: your sickness . . . your name . . . who you really *are*!"

The boys looked at her in surprise.

Nadia yanked her backpack from under the bed

and pulled out the identification cards. "You are one of *them*!"

"What are you talking about?" asked Tarek, staring in confusion at the cards she'd tossed on the quilt.

Nadia snatched one up and handed it to him. "Read it," she whispered harshly.

"'Ahmed Mazen Makhlouf,'" read Tarek. He paused and uttered the next line. "'*Mukhabarat* Commander.'" Shock registered on his face and he stepped away from the bed.

"You are *mukhabarat*?" said Basel.

Ammo Mazen looked at them with weary eyes. "Yes, at one time, I was."

"Why have you been lying to us?" asked Nadia, tears running down her cheeks.

He looked at her with a steady gaze. "I have never lied to you, or to anyone else," he said, a pained look on his face. "All the people who need to know, know who I am. They understand who I was, and who I became—a product of the choices I've made in my life."

"But how is this true?" asked Tarek, still staring at the card.

"I was born in Qardaha, in the northwest mountains, on my family's farm," he began, eyes drifting off as if he were looking out over a grove of oranges.

"As an Alawite, I was granted many privileges when Hafez came to power," he continued. "I was a young man, hoping to help build a bright new Syria."

"You were a part of those who ruled over the rest of the country with an iron fist," said Nadia, the words she'd been hoarding in her heart spilling out.

"The country had been in turmoil since the French left, and Hafez brought unity," said Ammo Mazen, ignoring her outburst. "In the beginning, I was caught up in the glory of the moment, of the endless possibilities."

"But you're not with them . . . the *mukhabarat* . . . now?" asked Basel.

"No," said Ammo Mazen. "As Hafez established absolute power, allowing injustice, inhumanity, and corruption to seep like poison into the country I loved so much, I could no longer do what was expected of me."

"Then what did you do?" asked Nadia. What she wanted to ask was *Who are you now?*

Ammo Mazen caught Nadia's troubled gaze. "I

left the *mukhabarat* nearly forty years ago," he said. "Tainted by their terrible work, I pretended I was ill and retreated into books, where there existed new worlds, people, and ideas."

He began to cough, and Tarek gently helped him sip from the cup of water.

"Thank you, son," he said with a grimace. "Soon after, I stumbled upon a path that led me to become a book repairer. And with my cart, I traveled to every corner of Haleb, meeting historians, bishops, professors, shopkeepers, beggars, archaeologists, and common folk. And as I grew to know them better, they shared their worries with me: a doctor couldn't find foreign-made medicines he desperately needed, a journalist required a reliable source for her story on government corruption, a taxi driver's son had been taken by the *mukhabarat* and he couldn't find which prison he was in. Whenever I could, I used my network of contacts within the secret police, government, and army to help such people find the goods or information they needed."

"That's amazing," said Basel, eyes wide.

The scorching anger that had flared within Nadia

fizzled, leaving the deep affection that had grown over the past few days. He was a gentle old man who'd spent his life helping people. A man who decided to take a lost girl and two orphans to safety.

"I'm sorry . . . ," Nadia whispered, collapsing beside the bed as she finally learned the reality of who the old man was. "Sorry that I believed the worst."

"It's not your fault, dear girl." Ammo Mazen smiled. "I'm afraid I'm a man who has learned not to reveal much."

"You are Ammo Mazen, no one else," she said.

Tarek took the old man's hands and knelt down. "*Allah* forgives all those who repent the past and pursue what is good."

"Yes," said Ammo Mazen. He looked at Nadia with haunted eyes, about to say something else, but then Umm Anous burst through the door. She stood panting. "You must go now. The black flags of ISIS are headed this way. They've taken the city of Azaz and are pressing their way east, battling competing rebel forces while the Syrian army moves in from the west."

"We'll be caught in the middle," blurted Tarek.

Nadia stared at Ammo Mazen, eyes pleading. "Please, come with us." She turned to Umm Anous. "It's not safe here," she said. "Everyone should come with us."

"No, my dears, our bones are too weary to leave." She laughed softly. "This is our land, our home. We will be buried here with our forefathers, in the dirt of Syria."

Basel stood holding his gun to his chest. "You have to come with us, sir," he whispered, tears running down his face. "There are doctors there that can help you."

"Children, time has finally caught up with me," said Ammo Mazen, his voice gentle. "My body is too weak to journey further."

"But we need you!" cried Nadia.

"My dear girl, do not weep," he said. "You have not needed me for a while now. You are much stronger than you think. And together, you three are more than capable of finishing your journey north."

Umm Anous nodded. "I will show you the safest path," she said. "If you leave now, you can follow the road along the valley's edge, hiding from the sight of the fighters. You will reach the border in a few hours."

"Go," said Ammo Mazen. "And take good care of Jamila for me."

Umm Anous was wrong. It didn't take a few hours to reach the border. It took over five, what with stumbling over rocky paths, the echo of gunfire and mortar rounds echoing around them. Twice they'd sought cover: once to avoid a troop of rebels and the second time when a group of refugees frightened them into a thicket of bushes. They'd skirted the town of Azaz a while ago, the black flags of ISIS fluttering against the brightening sky, the reek of diesel, gunpowder, and smoke carrying on the wind.

Jamila had periodically stopped, refusing to budge until coaxed with a soothing rub or a treat of tomatoes. Nadia knew how she felt. The faithful donkey had refused to leave Ammo Mazen's side, until he'd whispered something into her floppy ear. After a final nuzzle, the donkey had allowed herself to be led from the house, Ammo Mazen's last words ringing in Nadia's ears: *I was blessed to have been given the wisdom to leave the* mukhabarat. *I then chose to journey on a path filled with compassion and mercy. Now it is your turn—be wise in the choices you make.*

"Look," whispered Basel as they crested a hill, interrupting Nadia's thoughts, which lay back at the village with those they'd left behind. He pointed along a path. It was Kilis, the Turkish town bordering Syria.

"We made it," said Tarek. He muttered a prayer of thanks while cradling a grumpy Mishmish in his arms.

Nadia stood clutching Ammo Mazen's compass and staring in wonder at the road, crammed with exhausted, frightened souls. Most were on foot, but a few cars and buses inched along the asphalt. Up ahead rose the border between Syria and Turkey, delineated by towering white walls. At the end of the road rose the arched gateway, Bab al-Salama. Red, white, and black Syrian flags fluttered in the wind. *Father should be down there, on the Turkish side,* she thought, then frowned. The crowd was suddenly acting like a flock of spooked sheep that had seen a fox; something was wrong, and the caution she'd learned from Ammo Mazen kept her rooted to the spot.

"Let's go," said Tarek, but she held up a hand for them to wait.

Finally, Nadia realized what it was. "Who's manning the checkpoint?" she wondered out loud, staring at the gates on the Syrian side.

"No one," said Tarek, confused. "Didn't Umm Anous say the border was under rebel control?"

"Yes," said Nadia. Ten feet beyond the Syrian gate flew a duet of red flags, marked with a white crescent and star. *Turkey, Oncupinar border crossing. And Father,* thought Nadia, heart thumping against her rib cage as she squinted at the squat guard towers on either side of the gate. Turkish soldiers with rifles perched inside, overlooking the crossing. Beyond the gate she desperately sought a familiar figure, tall, lean, wearing a bulky olive-green coat. But from this distance, she couldn't make out the details of the people milling around beyond the gate.

Nadia double-checked the tarp to make sure it concealed whatever belongings they had left, including her backpack, which contained Ammo Mazen's black velvet bag of money. He had insisted they take it with them. "Let's go," said Nadia finally, ready to pull Jamila on, but Basel grabbed her arm.

"Wait," he said, staring at a battered truck parked upon a hilltop on the other side of the road. A familiar black flag flew from the back. *The flag of ISIS.*

"Oh no," whispered Tarek, surveying the length of the road that led back toward Syria. "There's another one," he added, pointing to an armored vehicle parked on the route to Azaz, flying the same flag.

"It looks like they've chased the rebels from the border crossing," said Nadia, now realizing why there were no rebels at the border. She eyed the men slouched in the back of the truck closest to them. A bedraggled family with crying children passed the truck, picking up their pace. The men in the truck observed them, but let them continue.

"They're not doing anything, just sitting there," muttered Basel.

"Maybe they were sent here from Azaz to keep watch and wait," conjectured Tarek.

"Wait for what?" asked Basel.

"To take over the border crossing," said Nadia.

"Then what are we waiting for?" squeaked Basel.

"Basel's right," said Tarek, placing Mishmish in his sack. "We need to get through before a battle breaks out, or they set up a checkpoint."

"Okay," said Nadia, adjusting her woolen cap. She

touched the silver brooch for good luck and started down the hill toward the road, pausing to let a truck full of exhausted families pass. Cautiously, they merged with other refugees, and made their way toward the gate.

"Don't look at them," whispered Basel, turning his face away as they passed the truck on the slope to the left.

But despite the terrifying stories she'd heard about them, how ISIS destroyed cities, looted ancient sites, and ruthlessly murdered anyone who disagreed with them, Nadia couldn't help but steal a glance. Instead of red-eyed, bloodthirsty barbarians, she found dusty, bedraggled men, many her brother's age, dozing in awkward positions. The ones that were awake sat bleary-eyed, staring at the flow of humanity passing by. Nadia blinked in wonder. *These are the fearsome ISIS warriors?* She focused on the border crossing, not realizing she was practically running as Jamila picked up speed, weaving through the crush of traffic.

"Nadia, slow down," Tarek called from behind.

"Jamila," Nadia cried, leaning over to wrap an arm around the neck of the agitated donkey.

"'Where is the beauty in a donkey?'" Nadia began to sing. "'The stumpy body, long ears? It's the heroic heart, stubbornness, and intellect behind the long-lashed eyes.'"

The intelligent animal blinked, slowing, and the boys caught up with them.

"We should go that way," said Basel, pointing toward a gap in the throng that wound its way toward the gate.

Nadia nodded, scanning the area along the fence delineating the border.

"Do you see him?" asked Basel hopefully.

Nadia shook her head as the crowd heaved forward, blocking her view of the gate. She peered through a gap between a group of girls and their mother, but could see nothing. Jamila brayed, uncomfortable in the crush. They slowed beside a group of drooping children standing with their parents near an idling bus. Further on stood an old man, leaning on a cane. Nadia's hip pressed up against the cart, sending a shooting pain down her leg.

The cart, she thought, and clambered on top.

"Good idea," called Tarek, climbing up beside her.

From her vantage point, Nadia scanned the gate, peering past Bab al-Salama toward the Turkish Oncupinar crossing.

"There are soldiers there," said Basel, pointing to a point beyond the guard tower. "And others . . ."

Nadia caught a flash of a man's bald head and grabbed Basel's hand. The man stood pressed against the gate, staring back into Syria, wearing a bulky olive-green coat that matched the cap on her head.

AUTHOR'S NOTE

On September 22, 2016, the Assad regime launched an offensive against rebel strongholds in Aleppo. Syrian troops, with the backing of Iran and Russia, pushed into the eastern part of the city, home to the famous *souqs* and the citadel through which Nadia journeyed. By the end of the year, only five percent of the territory remained in rebel hands, and a temporary ceasefire allowed citizens to be evacuated. A few weeks later, the Syrian army declared they had taken complete control of the city; Aleppo fell to the regime, giving the Syrian government control over one third of the country. Meanwhile, rebel groups, ISIS, and Kurdish forces continued to struggle for control over the rest of the country.

Reeling from six years of war, Syria is a fractured, broken country, its cities in ruins, its people deeply traumatized. The numbers are simply staggering. Since the conflict began, more than 450,000 Syrians have been killed, more than 1.8 million injured, and 12 million—half the country's prewar population—displaced from their homes as refugees.

In the winter of 2010, my family and I watched the news from Tunisia with fear and hope. It amazed us how Mohamed Bouazizi's suicide, in protest of mistreatment by corrupt government officials, sparked a regional revolution. But it was not really a surprise that he became the symbol of the frustration felt by millions across the Middle East; many lived under autocratic governments and desired a more democratic political system and a brighter economic future. News of Bouazizi's death spread like wildfire, amplified by technology and social media, in particular Facebook and Twitter. Tunisia fell to the will of the people within weeks, and the president fled the country. This buoyed the spirits of those in neighboring countries, and soon Tahrir Square in Cairo bulged with the suppressed fury of the Egyptians. Within months they too had toppled their dictator, and the fire, now called the Arab Spring, continued to spread across the region. My husband, who teaches Middle East politics, and I have lived and traveled in the region. Through our friends there, we heard firsthand accounts of the turmoil.

Finally, the flame reached Syria in February 2012, arriving at a time when the people were in the midst of economic hardship and social unrest. Frustrations were amplified as thousands of farmers flooded into the cities, trying to escape a multiyear drought, precipitated by climate change. It was in the city of Deraa, where a group of boys was arrested and tortured for spray-painting slogans against the government, that the fuse was lit. Emboldened, ordinary people flooded the streets in protest. The Syrian army retaliated with brutal force and a rebellion was born. At first it looked hopeful, but months turned into years and the bloody battles raged on, with hundreds of rebel factions defending their territories and ideologies. Although the initial protests were mostly nonsectarian, armed conflict led to the emergence of starker, sectarian divisions within the country.

And in war, it is the people who suffer. Who can forget the image of Aylan Kurdi, the tiny boy wearing a little red shirt, lying drowned on a Turkish beach? It was heartrending images of children fleeing the war that made me want to do something more than send aid and contact my ineffectual government representatives. I wanted to put a human face on the story unfolding before us. Sadly, Aylan reminded me of Mariam, from my first book, *Shooting Kabul*. When I finished that book, I felt that I had left one story unfinished, and that was the story of the little girl who is accidentally left behind by her family as they flee Kabul, Afghanistan. Although Mariam has a happy ending, the thought of what could happen to a child lost in a war lingered in the back of my mind. Nadia's story grew from there, with the hope of providing a window into the lives of the Syrian people, their country, and its history, arts, and culture.

ACKNOWLEDGMENTS

In writing Nadia's story, I felt a particular weight upon my shoulders. It was an emotional and creative challenge to address the complex, volatile issues of the Syrian war. My goal was to be as sensitive and accurate as I could, highlighting the beauty and resilience of the Syrian people in the face of adversity. I could not have written this book without the reporting of countless journalists who risked their lives working in Syria. Thank you for your stories and for generously allowing me to ask you questions. Per their request, I have withheld their names. *Escape from Aleppo* would not be here without an amazing literary team: my agent, Michael Bourret; and the incredible crew at Simon & Schuster—Paula Wiseman, my publisher; Sylvie Frank, my editor; Krista Vossen, art director; and the exceptional Education and Library team led by Michelle Fadlalla Leo. Much appreciation to my advisors on Syria: Lina Sergie Attar, Abe Kasbo, Rhonda Roumani, Sara Metz, Jamal Al Ani, and Razan and Mazen Asbahi. On notes of spirituality

I turned to Imam Tahir Anwar, who provided sage advice. And to my first line of readers—Hena Khan, Michelle Chew, and Carolyn and John Hackworth: you are awesome. And of course, never-ending thanks to Farid and Zakaria Senzai.

A READING GROUP GUIDE TO

Escape from Aleppo

By N. H. Senzai

About the Book

Twelve-year-old Nadia is much like any other preteen girl: She loves doing her nails and following the lives of television and pop music stars. Unlike most girls her age, Nadia is coming of age while a civil war rages inside her country of Syria. When the conflict arrives in her home city of Aleppo, her family makes a desperate attempt to flee and reunite with her father and uncles in a safer place. Then a bomb explodes and Nadia is separated from her family. She wakes up alone and unsure how to find the planned rendezvous location. She sets out on her own and happens upon a mysterious old man and his donkey. Although Nadia can't completely trust her newfound companion, she needs him to help her find her family and escape Aleppo to a new life in Turkey. *Escape from Aleppo* is a powerful story based on current events that reveals the complicated and dangerous situation in Syria, and the effects of the war on its citizens.

Discussion Questions

1. From the first page of *Escape from Aleppo*, the author uses sensory language to describe the atmosphere of violence and destruction in the Syrian city. As you read, place sticky notes on sections that create sensory imagery via descriptive language. Spend time discussing how the language brings the story to life.

2. Throughout the story, Nadia is gripped by anxiety. Discuss the meaning of the word and how Nadia copes with her feelings of fear and dread as she makes her way to the border between Syria and Turkey.

3. After Nadia realizes that her family has left her behind, she feels a deep sense of anger and betrayal, followed by a voice inside her head that says: "Get ahold of yourself. This is no time to fall apart. You must find the others." How does this internal dialogue propel the story forward? What does it tell you about Nadia's character? Discuss other examples of Nadia's internal dialogue and how they move the story forward.

4. Nadia witnesses a "sprawling park where a dozen rowdy kids roamed with joyful abandon." Nadia is "perplexed" and wonders how "they could be out playing in the middle of a war zone." Why do you think these kids are able to play so freely? How does this scene remind you of other times you've seen kids playing in a park? How is it different?

5. Memory is an important theme in *Escape from Aleppo*. How do Nadia's memories of life before the war help her persevere in her quest to find her family?

6. Discuss the role of social media, such as Facebook and Twitter, in the various Middle Eastern uprisings mentioned in the story. How can social media help to reveal the truth about authoritarian regimes? How can this openness also be used against those people who seek to overthrow such governments?

7. Nadia discovers Ammo Mazen in an abandoned pharmacy. After he agrees to help Nadia find the dentist's office, they enter into an uneasy partnership in which Nadia must weigh her need to find her family versus her feelings of mistrust for Ammo Mazen. As you read, stop and discuss instances in which Nadia must decide whether or not to trust the old man.

8. Throughout the story, Ammo Mazen demonstrates his compassion and commitment to reuniting Nadia with her family, and teaches Nadia about what is truly important in life. Discuss the meaning of Ammo Mazen's statements: "'I found that it is only by being a little lost that you stumble upon the path that is meant for you,'" and "'I've realized that every person's destiny leads them on a tumultuous journey. And if given bountiful blessings, how they choose to use them determines their humanity.'"

9. Ammo Mazen sings a song about the beauty in a donkey: heroic heart, stubbornness, and intellect behind long-lashed eyes. How can these qualities be considered beautiful? How does Nadia's definition of beauty change over the course of the story? How are her fingernails a metaphor for the change she undergoes over the course of the text? When she notices her chipped polish, she realizes she no longer cares about the appearance of her nails. Why?

10. Nadia is anxious to get to her family, but Ammo Mazen keeps delaying her quest to take care of his own business. She realizes that she "had to be patient, a virtue she was unfamiliar with." What is a virtue, and why is patience considered one? Give examples of how you demonstrate patience in your daily life.

11. Ammo Mazen laments, "'Thugs, our country has been overrun by ruthless thugs. From every side.'" Discuss the meanings of the words *ruthless* and *thug*. Cite examples from the book that illustrate Ammo Mazen's statement. Brainstorm synonyms for these two words and offer examples of thuggery. How are bullies and thugs similar?

12. Nadia realizes that Ammo Mazen has been working to save and preserve Syria's precious books. Discuss Professor Laila Safi's statement: "'My young soldier, this is the place where we are fighting a great battle.'" How is preserving cultural artifacts a battle? Why is it important to save such artifacts and landmarks? Other than the physical objects, what else is lost when cultural artifacts and landmarks are destroyed?

13. Discuss the meaning of the term *ethnic cleansing*. In the mind of an authoritarian leader, what is to be gained by committing such crimes against humanity? The author describes the Tunisian people as "throwing off the shackles of fear" and rising up "with demands for *aysh, hurriya, karama, adala ijtimáia*—bread, freedom, dignity, and social justice—and [beginning] a revolution." What is meant by "shackles of fear"? What is social justice? Discuss examples of social justice at work in the United States and other countries around the world.

14. Strength is another theme that appears throughout *Escape from Aleppo*. How does Nadia exhibit physical and emotional strength? How does her empathy for Basel encourage her strength in the darkest of moments? What is resolve? How does Nadia's strength and determination fuel her resolve?

15. Ammo Mazen gives Nadia the treasured copy of *Alef Layla, One Thousand and One Nights,* and says to her, "'I believe you have need of this more than a dusty old library or museum shelf does.'" What does Ammo Mazen mean by this statement? How do the stories contained in the book, such as "The Seven Voyages of Sinbad the Sailor" and "Aladdin's Wonderful Lamp," inspire Nadia to continue on? How is she like the story's heroine, Scheherazade?

16. When Nadia, Ammo Mazen, and the others come upon a group of journalists, Ammo Mazen says to Ayman, "'We need people like you to tell the truth of what is happening here.'" How are journalists who work in dangerous, war-torn regions heroic? Why do Assad and other dictators like him seek to control the news and stop journalists from doing their work?

17. Tarek is a student of the Quran, Islam's central holy book. In a conversation between Nadia, Ammo Mazen, Basel, and Tarek, Ammo Mazen points out that all people have "'been given free will to make choices on how we live our lives, and how we use the blessings given to us.'" He also says, "'It's in our hands, my dear. Always in our hands . . . to choose mercy and compassion, or be lost in a sea of inhumanity.'" What is free will? How does Nadia show mercy and compassion? How does the Assad regime demonstrate the opposite of mercy and compassion for the Syrian people?

18. Early in the story, Nadia's algebra teacher, Ms. Darwish, gives her a silver pin as a token of her belief in Nadia's potential and to reflect the idea of unlimited possibilities. After Ammo Mazen is attacked and Jamila taken, Nadia grips her silver pin and expects panic to embrace her. Instead, she "felt a strange sense of calm settle over her." How does the pin symbolize Nadia's growth over the course of the story? What has she been able to accomplish in only a few short days that she never would have imagined being able to do before she set out to find her family?

19. Discuss the scene where Nadia confronts Ammo Mazen about his real identity. Why does Nadia feel a sense of betrayal, even after everything Ammo Mazen has done to help her and the boys? What does Ammo Mazen mean when he says to Nadia, "'All the people who need to know, know who I am. They understand who I was, and who I became—a product of the choices I've made in my life.'" How do our choices affect the outcomes of our lives, for better or for worse?

20. On the book's final page, as Nadia and the boys approach the Turkish border crossing, she catches sight of a bald man "wearing a bulky olive-green coat that matched the cap on her head." Predict what will happen next for Nadia, Tarek, and Basel.

Extension Activities

1. Much has changed for Nadia since the beginning of the civil war. Create a Venn diagram illustrating Nadia's life before and after the Arab Spring, and what has remained a constant (her love for her family, etc).

2. The Middle East is one of the most volatile areas in the world, yet most young people are not familiar with the many countries that make up its geography. Print a map of the Middle East and consult an atlas or online research tools to identify the countries mentioned in *Escape from Aleppo*. Once these have been identified, trace Nadia's journey on the map.

3. Throughout the story, Nadia reads from *Alef Layla, One Thousand and One Nights*. Over the course of reading *Escape from Aleppo*, spend time each day reading aloud from this classic text.

4. The Syrian civil war has resulted in one of the worst refugee crises in history. Research the plight of Syrian refugees and how the world has responded to help these people.

5. Nadia and Basel come across an art installation of CDs "strung between the buildings and spelling out 'Art is peace'." Discuss the meaning of this phrase. Create an original work of art incorporating the same theme, "Art is peace."

Guide written by Colleen Carroll, literacy specialist, education consultant, and author of the twelve-volume series, How Artists See *and four-volume* How Artists See, Jr. *(Abbeville Press). Contact Colleen at about.me/colleencarroll.*

If you liked *Escape from Aleppo*, read on for a sample of *Ticket to India*, also by N. H. Senzai!

The moment they arrived, after an exhausting twenty-hour flight, they found the house, usually an oasis of calm, in chaos. Zara stumbled through the carved wooden doors first, while Maya entered last, sweaty from the soaring temperatures outside, a sharp contrast to cool, temperate San Francisco. She closed her eyes for a moment, watching a kaleidoscope of colors flash behind her eyelids—vibrant images that assaulted her senses each time she arrived. The sun seemed brighter here, more gold than yellow, raining heat down over the dusty city of Karachi. She opened her eyes and her pupils adjusted to the shadowy foyer, decorated in calming white, cream, and powder blue.

While her sister pushed past teary relatives to launch herself into her grandmother's arms with a dramatic sob, Maya stood back. She was stunned to see how her grandmother appeared to have aged a decade since she last saw her. Her usually meticulously wrapped sari was askew, and her silver hair, always pulled back in an elegant chignon, was wild around her shoulders. *Naniamma* had always been the strong, solid partner in her grandparents' marriage and Maya had never seen her cry, let alone fall apart like this. But as soon as *Naniamma* set eyes on Maya, she beckoned her for an enveloping hug. Before Maya could loosen her tongue and come up with something comforting to say, her mother gently pulled *Naniamma* away.

"Ammi," Dalia whispered, "I just can't believe *Abbu* is gone."

They clung to one another for a long minute, until a tight-lipped great-aunt guided them to the living room, with its ornate wooden sofas and embroidered cushions. As the adults and Zara huddled together, passing around a box of tissues, Maya stood, forgotten. Fighting the urge to hide under the dining room table as she had when she was a child, she spotted one of her grandfather's paintings hanging across from her, an abstract swirl of cool blues and beiges. She remembered the day he'd painted it, while on a picnic on Hawksbay beach. When he had been alive and healthy. Heart heavy, she slunk off with her backpack, up the stairs to the empty television lounge.

Longing to hear a comforting voice, she picked up the phone and dialed her home number in California. She wanted to tell her father that they'd reached Karachi safely. When the rings rolled over into voice mail, she realized he was probably out, dealing with burial plots, headstones, and other preparations for *Nanabba*'s funeral, which was to take place in San Francisco in a week. Restless, she went to the towering bookshelves that lined the room. She passed business, mathematics, poetry, and old novels, until she reached the section on history and politics. She pulled out a history book, titled *The Struggle for Pakistan*. On the way to the sofa, she switched on the television to a soap opera in Urdu. While her brain tried to adjust to a language she understood but didn't speak much, she glumly opened her backpack.

Sixth grade had started two weeks before, and Maya had been thrilled that her best friends, Olivia and Kavita, had been assigned to the same homeroom. But even before she could get used to a new class schedule, the news of her grandfather had come. And now, being away for more than a week meant completing take-home assignments: a stack of math sheets, a book report on Sacagawea, and a detailed journal describing her trip. With a sigh, she grabbed the journal like a lifeline, along with the new box of colored pencils she'd gotten for her art class. They'd just begun analyzing the works of the Mexican artist Frida Kahlo when she'd left for Pakistan. Frida's paintings were instantly recognizable by their bold, earthy colors—rainforest yellows, blood reds, vibrant blues, and neon pinks.

She flipped open the history book and froze. On the first page was a date, along with a signature: *Malik Humayun Ahmed.* Her grandfather. She stared at the blue ink, thinking back to a summer day, five years ago, when she'd gotten into a particularly nasty fight with Zara—over what, she couldn't remember. But it had ended how their fights usually did, with her sister throwing verbal daggers at her while she stood there mute, unable to formulate a good jab in response.

Later, it was *Nanabba* who'd coaxed Maya out of a tree and set up an easel for her in his office. Painting, for him, he'd explained, was like meditation. He'd shown her how to use a brush, demonstrating how the strokes could disentangle her thoughts. Each color, he told her, meant something different as it formed an image on the canvas. Red was danger, pink meant love, yellow hinted at cowardice, blue resonated calmness, green was renewal, and brown symbolized the earth. Maya fell in love with the process and later found that writing served the same purpose.

"And he was right." Maya sighed, writing a title on the front of her journal: "My Journey to Pakistan." On the next page she sketched a rectangular stretch of land, bordered by Afghanistan, India, China, and the Arabian Sea along the bottom. Then she began to write, soothed by the rush of words spreading across the page.

Thursday, September 15
Karachi, Pakistan

Here are some facts about Pakistan:

1. The name Pakistan—pak ("pure") and stan ("land") means "land of the pure" in the Persian and Urdu languages.

2. Islamabad is the capital, though Karachi is the biggest city.

3. The population is 193 million people, making

Pakistan the sixth most populous country in the world.

4. The national language is Urdu, the official language is English, and Saraiki, Punjabi, Pashto, Sindhi, and Baluchi are also spoken.

5. The official currency is the Pakistani rupee.

6. Cricket is the most popular sport.

My mom's family is from Karachi, Pakistan, but my dad was born in Chicago. His parents came to the United States from Pakistan in the 1970s so his father could get a PhD in engineering. As soon as he graduated, they moved to the West Coast and settled in Berkeley, California. My parents met when my dad went to Karachi to visit his grandparents. They liked each other instantly and decided to get married.

Maya paused. There was no avoiding it, she realized. Her grandfather was the reason they were here, and she had to say something about him.

The day before yesterday, my grandfather went to weed his garden in the cool part of the afternoon, as he usually did. A few hours later, that's where they found him, lying peacefully in a patch of tulips. He'd had a heart attack.

He was the eldest of three boys, and his greatest wish growing up was to fly. And so, even though his dad was totally against it, he became an air force pilot for the Pakistani military. But he didn't stay in the sky long. He came tumbling down to earth when he crashed during a training drill, and broke his back. His flying career over, he joined his father's accounting firm. When my grandfather told me this story, he wasn't sad. He just accepted what had happened as the will of God. He told me that as he buried his dream of flying, he uncovered something else—the joy of gardening.

My last memory is of him sitting on the porch, holding his pipe. I can still smell the smoke rising in the warm night air, mixed with the scent of musk and cedar wood—his Old Spice cologne. He'd been telling me one of my favorite stories about his childhood—about the time he and his best friend climbed up a mango tree and hung their schoolmaster's bicycle from its branches.

• • •

Maya exhaled a pent-up breath, the air rushing out of her lungs as her eyes filled with tears. She had been his favorite, she knew. He had never said it, but in his quiet, gentle way, he'd hinted at it as they both worked together on some shared interest or another—painting, gardening, collecting old coins, eating unripe mangoes sprinkled with chili pepper and salt. She clutched the journal to her chest and leaned back against the sofa, comforted by the words that were bringing her grandfather back to life, even if just for a moment.

Hot. It's really hot. Eyes flickering open, Maya found herself in a large four-poster bed with her sister sprawled beside her, a rumbling snore whistling through her nose. The window stood like a velvety black square, facing the garden. Jet-lagged, she must have conked out on the sofa and been moved here. She kicked off the too-warm blanket and sat up. *I should record her,* Maya thought gleefully, momentarily forgetting where she was. Her sister would have a conniption if she heard herself snoring. Maya sighed, staring at Zara's tranquil, pretty features, usually animated and full of life. But the momentary thought of embarrassing her popular, perfect sister filled her with quiet satisfaction—it hadn't been easy growing up as her younger sibling.

A junior at Berkeley High, Zara came home with straight As and had just been elected captain of the debate team. At Sunday school at the local mosque, the teachers were always perplexed that Maya was Zara's younger sister, since she couldn't memorize the passages from the Quran as fast as her older sister could. She'd wanted to reply that she took her time to analyze what she was memorizing to understand it better, but as usual, she couldn't muster the courage to do so. Maya's hands twisted the blanket. It wasn't as if Zara went out of her way to be mean to her—it was just so hard growing up in her shadow. Maya felt like she was forever trying to reach her, figuratively and literally, since Zara also towered a good foot above her.

Maya glanced at the clock on the side table, which glowed 5:23. A grumble below her belly button reminded her that she hadn't eaten any dinner. A particular eater—or "picky," as her sister would describe her—she stuck to the few things she liked. Right now, toast with jam sounded perfect. *It's nearly noon back home,* she thought. If only none of this had happened and she could be in school with her friends, huddled over a lunch of her usual cheddar and tomato sandwich. Slipping from bed, she headed downstairs, through the dark hall leading to the kitchen. She felt for the door, twisted the knob, and stepped inside—and was enveloped in a rush of icy air redolent with the scent of roses . . . *definitely not the kitchen.*

Illuminated by the small coffee table lamp lay *Nanabba*, wrapped in crisp white sheets, covered by garlands of his favorite flower, *Rosa bourboniana.* They'd been cut from his garden, where they were in full bloom, after a good soaking from the monsoon rains. The glorious pink roses filled every nook and cranny of the small sitting room. In the morning he'd be taken to the morgue, then fly back with them to San Francisco to be buried. Her gaze fixed on the body, she crossed the threshold, pulling the door closed behind her.